The Hired Bride

By
Carlotta Brittinger

PublishAmerica
Baltimore

© 2003 by Carlotta Brittinger.
All rights reserved. No part of this book may be reproduced, stored in a retrieval system, or transmitted in any form or by any means without the prior written permission of the publishers, except by a reviewer who may quote brief passages in a review to be printed in a newspaper, magazine, or journal.

First printing

ISBN: 1-4137-0510-3
PUBLISHED BY PUBLISHAMERICA, LLLP
www.publishamerica.com
Baltimore

Printed in the United States of America

For Heinz and Travis,
for keeping me grounded yet allowing me to soar.

ACKNOWLEDGEMENTS

The writing of this story took many months. It seems fitting, then, to pay tribute to those that have helped along the way.

And so, thank you to my sisters, Emma and Elaine, for their support and encouragement.

Sincere thanks go to Warren Evans for his guidance and advice.

I'm grateful to my mother and father who instilled in me, long ago, that I could reach for the sky.

A special thank you goes to Hannal for her unbridled enthusiasm – and for giving me my name.

To Warren –
Thank you!
Hugs,
Carlatta –
(Aysun)
x

Chapter 1:

Hartley Dale put his head in his hands and sighed. He swiveled around in his leather chair to stare moodily through the window. From his exquisitely furnished office on the nineteenth floor, he had a superb view of the city. He was not aware of it at this moment, however, for he was much more concerned with what was happening in his personal life than outside of it. He was being offered a most impressive position as Chief Executive Director of Farber Investments International Inc. It was no mean accomplishment to be offered this sterling position after only two years with the company, and an even greater achievement when it was considered that his background prior to this had not even been in the corporate world. It had been in an academic one. For three years, he was president of a university in western Canada.

He frowned and his dark eyebrows, thick and well-shaped met above his long straight nose. He turned back towards his desk and picked up a pen absent-mindedly. Suddenly, he flung his pen down and raked a well-manicured hand through his curly, dark brown hair.

A year ago he would never have believed there would be a doubt in his mind about accepting the new position. Yet now he was hesitant and extremely nervous. It was all because of Miranda – Burnett Farber's wife. As always, the thought of her filled him with desire and yet, the desire usually turned to anxiety when he realized that he had allowed her to place him in such an awkward position. What could be more uncomfortable than to be in love with the wife of the man you worked for, the man whose job you were being groomed to take over?

The door opened and his secretary came in. Bernadette was a petite, middle aged woman with a charming Irish brogue. He had inherited her along with this magnificent office.

"Come in Bernadette," he said when he saw her pause at the

door. "I've signed all the letters for tonight's mail. They are here in the out-tray."

She came over to his desk and picked up the folder marked 'for signature'. Looking at her boss over her bifocals, she asked, "Will you need me any more this evening?"

"No thanks, Bernadette. I'll see you tomorrow."

"Are you going home anytime soon, Mr. Dale?" Bernadette was always concerned that Hartley worked too much.

"Just summoning up my strength for that series of meetings tomorrow."

Bernadette looked sternly at Hartley. "Don't you ever get tired of business all the time?" she asked.

"Nope. I love it," he replied.

She smiled and, murmuring good night, went out closing the door behind her.

Alone again, he reached for his ever-present glass of mineral water and took several sips in quick succession. How different his life today was from where it had been two years ago. He would be the first to admit that it was due to plain luck as much as ability. Without one, the other could often be meaningless. But it looked as though his luck had failed him today. He frowned again. His scowl was deeper this time and anyone watching him would have been surprised by it. Frequently, the media referred to him as being poker-faced. It was a description he reveled in and played up for all it was worth, knowing that the less he gave away of himself the stronger his position would be. How few people knew the man behind this mask? Some days, he wasn't even sure he knew himself.

Putting down the water, he swung around to the window once more. It was fully dark now and snow had begun to fall lightly. The nights were getting colder. The lights of the rush hour traffic covered the road below in a sprawling glow of brightness that moved forward slowly, inch by inch. In the dark pane of glass, his head and shoulders were reflected, hair dark and curly, his cheekbones wide and high. His mouth was full but most people wouldn't know because he kept it tightly pursed most of the time.

THE HIRED BRIDE

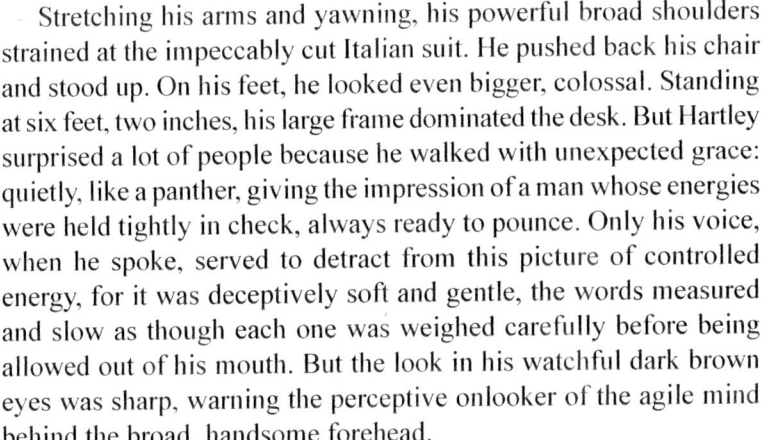

Stretching his arms and yawning, his powerful broad shoulders strained at the impeccably cut Italian suit. He pushed back his chair and stood up. On his feet, he looked even bigger, colossal. Standing at six feet, two inches, his large frame dominated the desk. But Hartley surprised a lot of people because he walked with unexpected grace: quietly, like a panther, giving the impression of a man whose energies were held tightly in check, always ready to pounce. Only his voice, when he spoke, served to detract from this picture of controlled energy, for it was deceptively soft and gentle, the words measured and slow as though each one was weighed carefully before being allowed out of his mouth. But the look in his watchful dark brown eyes was sharp, warning the perceptive onlooker of the agile mind behind the broad, handsome forehead.

There seemed to be no let-up in the traffic and he decided to wait a while before leaving the office. He thought of phoning down to the doorman to let his chauffeur know he would be delayed, and then decided against it. It was part of a chauffeur's job to wait. Waiting constantly must be incredibly tedious and he himself would have found it unendurable, but not all men thought as he did. Burnett Farber, for example, rarely considered other people. It was part of his strength that he cared a great deal only for the select few whom he believed to be necessary to the success of his company and his own personal happiness. Thank heaven I'm one of the select group, Hartley Dale mused. As always, the thought of Burnett Farber led to Burnett's wife. Though too young to be tied to a man approaching sixty-five years of age, she still carried her position with total ease, the way she handled everything - the same way she carried him into a situation that was now threatening to destroy his career.

Jamie's visit to him this afternoon had come as a shock and the content of his conversation even more so. But he had to decide what to do about it, even though he still had not settled on a solution. No, that wasn't true. He knew exactly what the solution should be – the only reason he was hesitating was because he knew that to do it would destroy everything he had worked for these past two years.

Two years. He glanced around his office, enjoying the rich, tasteful furnishings and the thick carpeting, the décor and the select, expensive pictures on the wall. It was Miranda's taste, of course, since she was the one who had the office decorated for him. It was supposed to be a gift from both herself and Burnett. But she had put her love into it – a love which he believed only he knew about until he discovered that Jamie knew too. God only knew how, but he did.

There was a light knock at the door and he turned around as it opened. A woman stood there, looking elegant with her tall, slim figure and full head of luxurious shiny copper-red hair. As always when he saw Miranda, he was struck by her exquisite beauty and the way every part of her blended into one graceful picture: the delicate features, full soft mouth and large blue eyes; the fluid way which she walked, moving her hips slowly from side to side, always perfectly groomed.

"Still working?" she said softly, closing the door and coming further into the room.

"You look so beautiful Miranda."

"What a lovely compliment to receive. That warms me up on this cold November evening."

She came closer still, almost face to face, but did not kiss him. They had always been careful when they met in the offices of Farber Investments, determined never to give anyone a chance to gossip. Yet Jamie had still found out. Again Hartley wondered how. Either he or Miranda had been careless. If Jamie knew, did anyone else?

"I just dropped by to congratulate you," Miranda sat down and crossed one ankle behind the other.

It was a practiced gesture, the way most of her gestures were, but Hartley drew pleasure from the slender ankles in hand-made leather shoes. Not a penny less than three hundred dollars, those shoes. He pushed the thought aside, irritated for even thinking it. What did money matter to him when he could now afford not to count it? But would that last? What would happen to him if Jamie carried out his threat and told Burnett that the man whom he had asked to be his Chief Executive Director was also in love with his wife?

"Miranda? We have a problem. We've slipped up somehow. Our

secret is out."

Miranda stared at him, still calm. "You mean Burnett knows?"

"No, not yet. It's your husband's nephew Jamie." He longed to take her into his arms.

Her blue eyes widened and she took in a quick breath. "James? But how? We've always been so careful. I've told no one. I swear it."

"Yes, well I would have sworn it too until about three o'clock this afternoon. That's when he came to see me. I thought it was to congratulate me on the new position but it was to issue an ultimatum."

"What do you mean?"

"Your nephew by marriage, has given me a choice," Hartley said heavily. "Either I give up on our relationship or he will tell Uncle Burnett all about us."

"He would never do that! Jamie knows very well that the shock of that would kill Burnett. It's the very reason *we* haven't told him." Clearly agitated now, she jumped up and came to stand beside him. It was an effort to stop himself from pulling her into his arms and smothering her face with kisses. But he knew he must not touch her unless they were absolutely certain that they were alone. It was a rule that had never been broken ... but now, it seemed that all of their careful planning had been for nothing.

"How on earth did he find out?" Miranda asked.

"I'm not sure. What he did say was that no one else knew – for now. He would be prepared to keep quiet about it either if I stopped seeing you or ..." Hartley picked up a gold pen and twirled it between his fingers.

"Or what?" Miranda pressed.

"Or turn down Burnett's offer of becoming Chief Executive Director."

"You can't turn it down! You're the only one capable of doing that job. It's what you've been working for!"

"Then are you suggesting that I give *you* up?" He tried to make his words sound light, but he knew he was fooling no one. He loved Miranda more than he had ever loved any woman. It was unthinkable to give her up. If only Burnett didn't have such a bad heart condition. If it hadn't been for that, he and Miranda would never have had to live this lie. If it hadn't been for his poor health, they would have told him a year ago. But they were both afraid of what the shock of the news would do to Burnett. That prevented them from taking the final step. Even now, he knew that, if given the choice, he would rather have Miranda than the plum job that had been offered to him. He had sufficient belief in his ability to know he could always find another ladder to climb. But he could not find another Miranda. It had taken him thirty-four years to find this one.

"We'll have to tell Jamie that we'll stop seeing each other," Miranda sat down again in her chair on the other side of the desk. "It might be a good idea if I talked to him too." Her beautifully arched red-gold eyebrows met together in a frown. "Are you absolutely sure that he knows about us – that it wasn't just an inspired guess?"

"Well, there was no guesswork in what he said to me." Hartley flung the pen down onto the desk. "He knew that we were together the same weekend that Burnett went into the clinic. He knows that we usually meet on Thursday afternoons."

"Who on earth told him? I wonder if it could be my maid?" Miranda's beautiful blue eyes darkened. "I'll fire her at once! I'll make sure she never works again."

Against his will, Hartley laughed out loud. "Well, I'll have to find another job too. Perhaps I could work as your maid."

He leaned forward with his elbows on the desk. "I don't suppose you would care to get divorced from Burnett and marry me? Hmm?"

"You know that I can't, Hartley." She leaned forward and the perfume that had become all too familiar to him wafted across the desk, intoxicating him with the warm fragrance. "If Burnett was not such a sick man, I would have left him over a year ago – when we fell in love with each other."

"Would you have Miranda? I'm not sure about that. Sometimes I think that you've become far too comfortable in your life with him. The money, the servants....it would be difficult to leave all that."

"How can you say that?" Forgetting that they were normally

careful when they were in the Farber Building, she came to his side of the desk and hugged him tightly. "I love you Hartley. If I didn't, I never would have put myself in this position. Do you think I enjoy all the secrecy – the sneaking around? The pretence and lies that we have to tell? I am so afraid when you speak like this, my love."

"Afraid of what?"

"That you don't want me any more!"

"Don't want you!" His voice became loud and Miranda held a finger to his lips. "I want you so much that sometimes I can't think straight. You've gotten under my skin."

"Sometimes I feel that you hate me because of it."

"Never!" he said vehemently. "I love you. I love you Miranda." He pulled her close but when he bent to kiss her, she turned her head away. "What's it to be?" he asked, forcing his mind away from her soft skin and back to the problem at hand. "If you won't tell Burnett – and I can understand why – then I have no choice but to resign and look for a position elsewhere."

Immediately she looked up at him, her eyes moist with tears. "You can't do that. I won't let you destroy your career because of me. Let me talk to Jamie."

"You won't get him to change his mind. I tried this afternoon. He was adamant."

"Have you thought about what Burnett will say when you tell him you don't want to be Chief Executive Director?"

"I hadn't thought that far ahead yet," admitted Hartley.

"Then it's time you did," Miranda pulled herself away from his embrace and went back to her chair, in control again. "And it's time that Jamie did too. Ask him to come and see us."

"Right now?" Hartley was surprised.

"Why not? The longer you allow a bad situation to ferment, the worse it will get. Jamie has made a threat and we have to discuss it."

"Are you suggesting that we stop seeing each other?"

"As far as our young James is concerned, yes. We wouldn't really of course, but …"

"It won't work Miranda. If he could find out about us in the first place, he would soon discover that we were trying to fool him."

"Not if I get rid of my maid. I'm sure he paid her to spy on me. He has always hated me since the day that I married his uncle."

"That is understandable. He was afraid that you would have children and deplete his inheritance."

Miranda stared coldly at him. Hartley cursed himself for having spoken. "I'm sorry. I know how you feel about not having any children. Forgive me."

"I don't think you do know. If I had known that Burnett couldn't make me pregnant, I never would have married him," she said evenly.

"It was crazy to marry him anyway, in my opinion," Hartley replied. "He's old enough to be your father."

"Try and understand," she explained. "He was charming and sophisticated and I was very young, just out of university. He showered me with expensive gifts, trips, designer clothing, and jewelry …all the things that impress young girls."

"Weren't there any younger men who were willing to do the same?"

"None of them had Burnett's charm," Miranda sighed. "And of course my father knew him in New York and you know what a world of its own New York is, with Burnett one of the ruling princes. I suppose that turned my head more than anything else."

It was a story Hartley had heard before and, as always, he thought that it was a waste of this lovely, vital woman's charms. Being tied to a man thirty-five years her senior had taken much of her strength and energy especially in the past year since Burnett's health had deteriorated so rapidly. Her parents must have been crazy to give their blessing to this marriage, though gossip was that they had used their daughter's beauty as a financial asset. Yet even marriage to Burnett Farber could have been broken if it was not for his ill health.

"Burnett isn't getting any better Hartley," Miranda whispered. "He went for a check-up the other day and I spoke to his physician afterwards. He told me that it's just a question of time."

"Baloney!" Hartley replied. "If he takes life easy, he can go on for many years."

"He won't go on for years. You know that's a fact as well as I do. That's why we have to be patient and bide our time."

"And how do we keep Jamie quiet in the meanwhile?" Hartley asked.

"I don't know," she sighed as she looked at the telephone. "It seems strange to admit to someone about us. Do you know that Jamie will be the first person I've ever discussed it with?"

"The way I feel, I would like to shout it from the rooftops," Hartley said, and then chuckled. "You make me feel like a teenager sometimes."

"You don't act like one," she said huskily, holding out her hand towards him. "Are you free this weekend, my love? Burnett is going into the clinic again."

"I'm always free," he reminded her. "You are the one who finds it difficult to get away."

Ignoring his comment, Miranda pointed to the telephone again and he picked it up and punched in James Farber's direct line.

"I would like to see you in my office at once," he said to the younger man and then replaced the telephone without waiting for a reply. "Well," he turned to Miranda, "have you worked out what you're going to say to him?"

"Not yet. But not to worry – I'm a very good musician and I'll play it by ear."

A few minutes later as he walked into Hartley's office, Jamie's naturally pale face grew paler as he noticed Miranda sitting there. "Hullo Miranda," he said stiltedly.

"James," Miranda replied in her softest tone. "Hartley has just told me that you've discovered a secret about us."

Jamie looked nonplussed, as if he had not expected such a frank admission of their relationship.

"There's no point in the three of us pretending," Miranda continued. "Now that you know the truth, you've become part of the secret. A cozy little triangle you might say." She paused. "Unless you've told someone else?"

"No one," Jamie replied. "It isn't something I'd care to talk about."

"I don't care to talk about it either, but you've made it impossible for me not to do so."

"I don't want to cause you any trouble, Miranda," Jamie said quickly. "I'm only concerned with Uncle Burnett."

"Do you think I'm not concerned with Burnett too? Why else do you think I've stayed with him these past seven years?"

"You're his wife, that's why. Why shouldn't you stay with him?"

"Because he isn't my husband – not in a physical sense anyway. We haven't lived as husband and wife since the year after we were married!"

Deep color stained Jamie's cheeks, making him look younger than his twenty-eight years. "I'm sorry. I had no idea."

"Why should you have? It isn't something one would broadcast."

"Please don't say any more. Your private life is your b…"

"Your business now Jamie," Miranda interrupted. "You've made my affairs your business, so the least you can do is stand there and listen to the whole story. Your uncle has been ill for a long time. It affected our physical life together long before his illness became publicly known. If I'd been tougher, I would have left him then. He offered to divorce me, you know, but because I loved him as a person I couldn't bring myself to hurt him. So I stayed and tried to make myself believe that I could live without love – without the happiness that comes with all things in a relationship. Physical, emotional and spiritual love." She paused and glanced at the man standing behind the desk. "And I did live without it – until I met Hartley."

"Do you think it's necessary to tell Jamie all these details?" Hartley's voice was hard.

"Yes, I agree," Jamie added. "I don't need to know the whole story. I don't want to know!"

"I'm trying to make you understand why I fell in love with Hartley. It wasn't because I had stopped loving Burnett." She looked directly at Jamie again. "My feelings for your uncle remain unchanged. I never wanted to hurt him, and I still don't."

"Well, neither do I," Jamie said.

"But you're threatening to tell him about Hartley and myself.

And that will hurt him very much."

Jamie shook his head. "Are you blind? He's bound to find out sooner or later."

"He hasn't so far."

"Because up until now, you've been careful. But in the last few months you haven't. How do you think I found out?"

"How did you?" Miranda asked. "I've been very curious about that."

"I was delivering some documents to Hartley's penthouse one evening. Instead of leaving them with the security desk, I went up to talk to him. Security knows me so they didn't even blink an eye. I needed his advice on one transaction. I heard your voice behind the door, Miranda." He paused uncomfortably and then braced his shoulders. "You were calling out something to Hartley and it was pretty obvious that you two were much more than just friends."

Hartley thought back to the one and only time – about a month ago – when Miranda had come to his place. Always until then they had chosen their meeting places with discretion, but the week before he had been out of town and upon his return, their need to see each other had been so great that it had overcome their normal caution. He was furious and he longed to get up and grab Jamie by the throat. Swallowing hard, he forced himself to remain calm. A display of violence could only do more harm than good.

"Why destroy Hartley's career?" Miranda said. "I am as much to blame as he is."

"I don't happen to agree."

Jamie shot Hartley a look of anger and he returned it in kind. It was just as he thought. Jamie was jealous of him – of his success with women and in particular with Miranda. Perhaps he even loved her himself and had entertained hopes of being with her when his uncle died. It was an interesting thought and he wondered how Jamie would react if he mentioned it. For the moment he decided to hold his peace but would keep that card up his sleeve.

"Jamie, listen to me. If Hartley turns down Burnett's offer, he'll have to give him a damn good reason," Miranda said.

"I'm sure he can think of one."

"He will also be available to seek a new position with one of our rivals," she added.

"So what?"

"So, how do you think your uncle will react to that? Burnett has been grooming Hartley to become Chief Executive Director. He has told him all the plans he has for the company – confidential plans which no one else but Burnett and Hartley know about – so what sort of loyalty do you expect Hartley to have towards Farber Investments International if you force him to leave?"

Jamie groaned and placed both of his palms against his forehead in exasperation. During Miranda's speech, he had grown more and more agitated and he was not master of his own emotions. He couldn't hide his annoyance.

"You hadn't thought of that, had you?" Miranda pursued him relentlessly. "You just thought you could go to a man like Hartley and blackmail him into doing what you wanted?"

"I am doing it to protect my uncle!"

"By getting rid of the one person who can take all of this responsibility off his shoulders?" Miranda's voice was clear and even as she defied Jamie to tell her what she had said was untrue.

But he ignored the question, and answered it with another one. "Don't you think my uncle can find someone else? Hartley Dale isn't irreplaceable."

"Well, Burnett wouldn't agree with you. He searched for three years before he found Hartley and it has taken him another two years to groom him for the position. Do you honestly think he can find someone else?"

"In time he will."

"Time is the one thing that your uncle hasn't got Jamie! For heaven's sake, be logical."

"I am trying to be," he burst out. "But all I can think of is you and Hartley making a fool of my uncle. How do you think he would feel if he found out about your affair?"

"He won't find out, unless you tell him."

"Sooner or later someone else is bound to know," Jamie shook his head. "That's why you have to stop it now."

"And if we refuse?" Hartley intervened.

"I will tell my uncle the truth."

"Then I have no other choice but to leave the company. I have no intention of giving up Miranda."

"You can't leave!" Miranda cried out. "What on earth will you tell Burnett?" She glared at Jamie. "Get this through your head James! Burnett regards Hartley as a member of his family. If Hartley goes, then he'll think he is reneging on his promise."

Jamie lowered his head and stared down at the carpet. "There is only one way that would make it possible," he said, looking up. "You would both have to promise to end your affair."

Hartley opened his mouth to speak, but saw a warning look in Miranda's eyes. He closed his mouth again. Not sure what she wanted to tell him, he remained silent. He stood still, waiting for Miranda to speak.

"If Hartley and I give you that promise," Miranda murmured, "does that mean you will say nothing to Burnett?"

Jamie hesitated, locking eyes with Miranda. "Well, I would require more than just a promise."

"What do you mean?"

"I wouldn't just take your word for it. Do you think I'm that naïve?" Jamie glared at Hartley. "I would need some proof."

With great effort, Hartley controlled his temper, though the urge to smash his fist into Jamie's baby face was overwhelming.

But his voice was mild. "And how am I supposed to give you proof that I have – that I'm not seeing Miranda?"

"By marrying someone else." Jamie looked from Hartley to Miranda, triumphant in the knowledge that he had succeeded in overtaking the lead in this little scene. "Well," he asked. "What is your decision?"

Hartley stared into Miranda's eyes. Though they burned with blue intensity, he could not read any meaning in them, and he swung around on the young man. "I'll be damned if I'll let you dictate to me. Your uncle is a sick man. At the most he has a couple of years left to live. You're crazy if you think I'll tie myself to another woman. As soon as Miranda is free, we *will* get married. I would marry her tomorrow if she'd say the word."

"I'm not interested in the least about your future with Miranda," Jamie said bluntly. "My only concern is for my uncle's happiness in the time that he has left on this earth. As of this moment, Hartley, you are the one who is threatening it. If you don't want to resign or get out of Miranda's life, then the only alternative – "

"Give us some time to think about it," Miranda interrupted.

"What?" Hartley looked at her.

"How much time?" Jamie asked. "Uncle Burnett is making a statement about Hartley to the press tomorrow afternoon. If Hartley is going to turn down the offer …"

"We will decide before tomorrow afternoon. The quicker you leave us alone to discuss this, the quicker we will make our decision."

Jamie went to the door. "Please don't think for a moment that I want to hurt either of you. But Uncle Burnett brought me up and well, he is like a father to me."

"Spare me the mawkish sentiments!" Hartley growled. "Now get out and leave us alone."

Chapter 2:

Claire Evans jumped off the bus as it pulled into the Bayview Avenue stop near the Granite Club. She set off briskly north towards the Bridle Path. Bayview was always such a busy street, with drivers speeding remorselessly past her.

The noisy street contrasted greatly from the calm elegance of the huge homes in this elite part of the city. Seeing a gap in the traffic, she took the opportunity to jog across the street and disappear into the quiet, exclusive neighborhood. The whole area was well known as the most expensive in Toronto. The price of the smaller houses started at almost two million dollars. It was not unusual to find mammoth homes worth six or seven times that amount, sitting on an acre or more of luxurious, gardener-maintained property. It was here that Miranda lived with her wealthy husband Burnett Farber.

Claire mounted the steps and rang the doorbell. She always felt nervous coming to this home, a throwback to her years as a poor, university student. Both she and Miranda had gone to York University to study. Miranda had always been the confidant one; the one in control. Claire had always felt so many years younger even though Miranda was twenty-nine and Claire twenty-seven.

"Good evening, Harriet," Claire greeted the maid as she stepped into the light, marble-floored foyer. "Mrs. Farber is expecting me."

The maid nodded and took her coat and she went upstairs, past the first floor and the drawing room to the second floor with its two enormous master bedrooms, each with its own sitting room, fireplace and ensuite bathroom. It was the huge room on the left that she entered, and stopped because Miranda was not there.

"I'll be with you in just a second," Miranda called out from her walk-in closet/dressing room. "I got back late and I'm changing into something comfortable. Help yourself to some wine from the bar."

"No thanks," Claire answered in a light firm voice. "I've typed all your letters. Are there any new ones?"

"They are on the desk Claire. But hold on – I want to talk to you for a moment."

Claire wandered over to look at the mound of open envelopes on the mahogany desk, then remembering Miranda's orders, went over to sift through a pile of the latest fashion magazines stacked on one of the tables. Seeing nothing of interest, she wandered over to the floor-to-ceiling window which overlooked the small garden. In the summer, it was filled with tubs of exotic flowers and small, perfectly manicured trees. Right now, it was shrouded in November gloom.

She caught herself in the vanity mirror as she backed away from the window. Claire Evans was a dark-haired, sad looking young woman. She was only five feet, two inches tall with a small delicately boned frame and a pale, creamy complexion. Her jet black hair fell thick and straight to her shoulders. Her nose was slightly tilted and her chin was small, but firm and determined. Without a doubt, her eyes were her most beautiful feature. They were a beautiful gray – wolf's eyes her cousin called them. Above them were long, dark winged eyelashes. She felt that her eyes gave away so much of her emotion so she generally kept her lids half lowered, a habit she had developed during her years at university. She had a small, soft full mouth which was beautiful, but she kept her lips pursed most of the time. Too much sadness on her face, she thought. Since her parents' untimely death which had occurred the year before she graduated, there had been little in her life to make her happy.

Miranda's entrance was a welcome interruption to her unpleasant memories and Claire greeted her with a warm smile. Miranda would have been surprised to know that Claire saw through her charm to the selfishness that lay beneath it. She would have been even more surprised to know that Claire actually liked her because of it, admiring the ruthless tenacity with which she achieved what she wanted.

"Forgive me for taking so long," Miranda said, bending down to kiss her friend on the cheek. The warm tone and the affectionate greeting warned Claire that a favor was going to be asked of her.

"Oh no, Miranda. I hope you don't want me to fill a vacant spot at one of your boring dinner parties?"

"Claire! How can you call them boring? Some of the most interesting people in the whole country come here to dine."

"It takes more than a fat bank account to make people interesting to me."

"I swear to God, Claire! You're a secret socialist."

"Not such a big secret Miranda," Claire grinned and looked so young and unsophisticated in her navy pants and over-sized white sweater.

"Don't you have something more stylish to wear?" Miranda asked. "You look about sixteen in that outfit."

"Beggars can't be choosers," Claire retorted, and added quickly, "and don't offer to lend me any money because you know I'll refuse it."

"It's so foolish Claire! If you prefer to give your money to that no-good cousin of yours, then …"

"Charles has been like a brother to me," Claire interrupted.

"Just because you two grew up together?" Miranda stopped herself. She realized that to minimize Claire's loyalty to her cousin was exactly the opposite of what she wanted to do. It was this loyalty that she was counting on for the success of her plan. "Any hope of Charles paying off his debts?"

"Not unless a miracle happens within the next couple of months."

"And if he doesn't?"

"I don't really know. He'll probably go to jail, I suppose. The auditors will start examining the company books right after Christmas. January is the end of their fiscal year. Charles says they will spot the discrepancy within a few weeks."

"So unless he can re-pay that forty thousand dollars, they will discover that he stole it?" Miranda emphasized the point.

"He didn't steal it Miranda," Claire protested. "He borrowed it to invest in the stock market. He had no idea that the market would take such a bad downturn."

"Hmmm…well, there's a nasty name for people who take other people's money," Miranda said. "Face it, Claire. Your cousin is a thief and he's not even a very good one. But if you feel so obligated to him that you're willing to live like a little church mouse in order to give him every penny that you have..."

"You will never understand. He was so respectful and caring to my parents," Claire explained, "and wonderful to me when they died. It wasn't easy for him to be saddled with a shy, weepy nineteen-year-old who had never been on her own before. I needed help and he was there for me. He also paid for me to finish my last year at university. I would never have gotten my degree without him. You know that."

"You've repaid him for that, Claire."

"You can never repay a person for this kind of support and benevolence. You have to go on doing it. He's in trouble now and he needs my help. It's give and take, Miranda. Not just take!"

"Better you than me," Miranda shrugged. "But then I'm not the self-sacrificing type." She drifted across the room in a cloud of expensive perfume. Beautiful copper-gold hair lay long and curly against her neck and shoulders. Looking at her, Claire wished she too possessed such gilded beauty and, with a pang, pushed the thought aside.

"What is it that you wanted to discuss with me, Miranda?"

"Sit down Claire and relax. What I have to say will take a little time." Her beautiful mouth curved into a smile. "You've heard me speak of Hartley Dale?"

"The handsome rising star of Farber Investments?" Claire rolled her eyes. "Um... yes a few times."

Miranda ignored the sarcastic tone. "He needs your help. Burnett has asked him to become the Chief Executive Director – it will be announced officially tomorrow. Naturally I'm delighted because it takes a lot of the responsibility away from Burnett. Eventually, I'm hoping that Burnett will retire completely."

"Well, he should have retired ages ago. It's not as if he needs the money Miranda."

"Men like Burnett don't work for money," Miranda grinned. "They do it for the prestige and power."

"Then they're crazy." Claire gave a shake of her head. "Go on.

Sorry I interrupted you."

"I was talking about Hartley. In his new position he will have to do a great deal of entertaining – people from all over the world, financiers – and he'll need someone to assist him in all that."

"Well that's not a problem. I'm quite willing to do that as long as he doesn't expect me to be on call every single weekend."

"This isn't just a weekend job," Miranda said. "It's a full time one."

Slowly raising her eyebrows, Claire stared at Miranda.

"Hartley isn't looking for an assistant, Claire."

Claire blinked once.

"He wants a wife."

Miranda disliked being involved in the situation in which she found herself that afternoon with Jamie. She hated not being in control yet there she was, faced with the most dramatic decision of her life with little chance of maneuvering it, the way she normally was able to bend and mold everything that was important to her. All because that little weasel Jamie had delivered some damn documents to Hartley's penthouse a month ago.

She wanted to jump up and scream – to shout and flail her arms about. But the habit of years of practice kept her sitting calmly in the chair in Hartley's office, hands in her lap, looking for all the world as if she did not have a single worry in the world. She dared not let Hartley go to another company. Not because she was afraid he might give Farber secrets away – which she had allowed Jamie to believe – but because she feared that if he worked in a different office then he would form a social life in which she would play no significant role. More important still, if he no longer worked for Burnett he would no longer feel the same loyalty towards him. He would eventually give her an ultimatum - either she leave Burnett or he would end their love affair.

The first and only time Hartley had said this she had managed to talk him out of it, but it had not been easy, and she had to play on

Burnett's heart condition and his need of Hartley to run the company before she won her argument. Hartley's appointment as the new Chief Executive Director had made her feel that at last she could breathe more easily, for the very importance of his position would act as a brake on him, making him realize that to run away with the wife of the Chairman would do his reputation no good.

But now Jamie was threatening to destroy everything she had planned; not just the present comfortable position of her life – a multi-millionaire husband and a virile adoring lover – but her future too. Hartley was not an easy man to fool. It required constant vigilance to maintain his illusion of her. Sometimes she wondered what he would say if he knew that, far from staying with Burnett because she cared about this health, she was staying because she had given him seven long years, and intended to remain with him until he died and she inherited his fortune. How horrified Hartley would be if he knew how truly mercenary she was and how little sympathy he would have for her reasons. Never knowing the shame of having to pretend to be what you weren't – which her parents had done throughout her childhood – he had no conception of her obsessive need for financial security.

Yet as much as she wanted Burnett's money, she had no intention of giving up Hartley. More than any other man she had ever been with, and she had loved many, though he had no idea about this, she wanted him more than anyone else she had met in her life. From the moment Burnett had brought him to dinner and asked him to join Farber she had pictured herself as his wife, eventually. With Burnett's health failing she had thought it was only a matter of time before she and Hartley could openly declare their love, and things would have worked out as she had planned. If it hadn't been for Jamie! Fury made her tremble. How she longed to wrap her hands around his throat and throttle him.

But then she had a brilliant idea.

"Darling," Hartley had said, "there's no point in getting upset. It isn't the end of the world. Watson & Sons will be more than glad to take me; and they aren't Farber rivals."

"No!" She spat out. "I won't let you work for anyone else. This company is your future – our future."

"We won't have a future if I stay here," he said grimly. "Jamie isn't bluffing. He will tell Burnett. We cannot go on pretending any longer, Miranda."

"We could if you were married to someone else."

Hartley took a step back to look into her eyes. "Do you know what you're saying?"

She hesitated. The words had come out in a blunt way she had not planned on. But there they were. When Jamie first told them that the only way in which he would allow Hartley to remain as Chief Executive Director, she dismissed the idea. But now she was beginning to see merit in the suggestion. If she could marry Hartley to some hired hand who would remain his wife until she was free to marry him, she would be achieving two objectives. First, it would enable Hartley to stay on at Farber, and; second, it would tie him to a marriage of convenience to ensure that he was not free for anyone else.

But where would she find a young woman who was bright and attractive enough to be his temporary wife? It was not a job posting you could put in the newspaper. The tact and secrecy it required necessitated finding a young woman with loyalty, integrity and, most importantly, a pressing need for money.

Claire Evans! The name and the face flashed into her mind. That was it. The very person they needed.

"Marriage for you might just be the best way out," she said slowly. "Not a real marriage, of course, but a contractual arrangement." She was delighted at her choice of words, for they brought the discussion on to a business level instead of an emotional one. Hartley straightened up and stood beside the desk.

"It would solve all of our problems," she continued, "If you were to marry a quiet, smart, well-spoken woman then you could continue with your work here. I'm sure you don't want to give it up after all the effort you've put in – and we could go on seeing each other."

"Yes, and I could go on seeing you if I worked for Joseph Watson."

"Burnett would be far more suspicious then."

"So what?" Hartley said. "We wouldn't have the need to be secretive if I was no longer working here."

"We aren't keeping our love secret because you work here. It's because I don't want to hurt Burnett. My leaving him would kill him. You know that!"

Hartley wished he could deny it, but honesty would not let him. Burnett adored Miranda and to take her away from him could well be a shock from which he would never recover. "Then we will have to keep our affair a secret until…" He stopped, unable to say the words 'until Burnett dies' even though he knew they were implied. "But I can't go on working here. At least my leaving will ensure Jamie's silence. That's what we both want."

"How do you think Burnett will react to your leaving?" Miranda cried. "You can't throw his job back into his face and walk out. That would destroy him."

"Burnett isn't that easily destroyed by business setbacks."

"He wouldn't regard you going as a business setback but as a personal one. I wasn't lying when I told Jamie that Burnett looks upon you as his son."

Once again Hartley could not deny what Miranda had said. Yet neither could he consider marrying anyone else. He thought of the few women he had dated in the past year; not because he wanted another woman's company but because being seen with them helped to maintain the deception that he was a fun-loving bachelor. In his mind, every evening spent with another woman had been a wasted one. It only succeeded in making him realize that only one pair of lips could give him satisfaction. Only one body could assuage his needs.

"I will never marry anyone except you," he stated and, though he remained against the desk, their eyes met in a look that was all-embracing.

"It would only be a business arrangement," Miranda insisted.

"Like hiring a secretary?"

"Exactly."

"You can fire a secretary," he said, wryly.

"If you can make a proper agreement with the right person, you would also be able to end a marriage. Annul it," she added, perhaps too quickly.

Hartley could not help smiling. "You have no reason to be jealous of me. If I did marry a woman other than you, there would be no problem about getting an annulment based solely on the absence of any sexual relationship." He reached out and touched her hand. "You're the only woman I ever desire."

"Hartley," she whispered, and leaned her warm body against him knowing that when he felt her close it was more difficult to refuse her anything. "Can't you see this is the best way out? You could marry a suitable candidate who would go with you to all those boring functions you have to attend, and at the same time it would stop Burnett's fears about us. Best of all, it would cut the ground from under Jamie's feet!"

"Well that would be asking a lot of an employee," he said, counting on the fingers of one hand. "Allaying the fears of the suspecting husband, acting as my hostess on boring social occasions and cutting away the ground from under the feet of a little rat-boy."

"You're making fun of me," Miranda reproached.

"This is not a feasible situation. It's a pipe dream. I will not marry someone else. I'm going to call Joseph Watson's office tomorrow and set up an appointment with …"

"Please don't. I have a candidate in mind already. I'm sure she would be willing to do it. It would solve all our problems."

If hearing Miranda suggest that he marry someone else surprised Hartley, then hearing she actually had a candidate for the position surprised him even more. Seeing his expression, Miranda pressed home her advantage.

"It's a girlfriend of mine from university. We took a couple of the same courses together. She and I hit it off and I know she really liked me. I think she was a little envious." Miranda smiled. "We kept in touch after I had left school- a year before she did. We meet from time to time on birthdays, lunches and sometimes during Christmas holidays. For the past couple of years, she's helped me occasionally when I need a secretary. Also, if Burnett and I do a lot of entertaining she lends a hand with the arrangements. She's very efficient – and bright."

"What makes you think she'll be willing to sacrifice herself for us?

"She really needs the money."

"What money?" Hartley asked sharply.

"We have to pay her, Hartley. Who would enter into this contract without any payment?" Miranda explained. "I thought we could offer fifty thousand dollars on the day of the wedding and another fifty thousand dollars when the marriage is annulled. Not bad for a couple of years work – tax free!"

"Well, well," Hartley said softly, "So I've finally sunk so low as to finding it necessary to purchase a wife!"

"I'm trying to help you here!" Miranda was starting to get angry. "This is to help both of us."

"I'm sorry Miranda," he said pulling her into his arms. "It's just that I really can't take this idea seriously. I've thought about marrying *you* for so long that this plan seems ludicrous to me. I don't even want to think about it."

Hartley felt Miranda stiffen in his arms and prepare to move away. "Okay, tell me more about her."

"There isn't much to tell. We went to the same university. She had always been fond of me."

"I'm not surprised. I can just imagine you taking pity on some silly little buck-toothed girl with thick glasses. I bet you were the most beautiful student in the whole university."

"I never thought about my looks then," Miranda lied, "though I don't think Claire ever had buck teeth. I know she doesn't wear glasses."

"If I know anything about you, my darling, I know that the wife you would choose for me must look like the back of a bus!"

"Hartley. I'm surprised at you. I wouldn't choose an ugly wife for you. There has to be a logical reason for you wanting to marry her."

"Well, even ugly girls get married," Hartley said. "You put too much emphasis on appearance."

"Would you love me if you didn't find me beautiful?"

"The question is academic Miranda." His arm tightened around her. "I wouldn't love you if you were a fool, either. But I want to marry you – not anyone else."

"At least agree to meet her," Miranda insisted. "She's coming to the house tonight anyway. I know that Burnett has asked you to dinner and it would give you an opportunity to meet her." She gave him a quick hug and stepped away.

Hartley sighed and accepted the fact that Miranda was in no mood for his kisses. "What makes you so sure that this woman would agree to marry me? I know the money is a considerable attraction but even so…"

"The money is the main attraction. She needs it for a man."

If he had developed a faint liking for this unknown woman who loved his Miranda, it evaporated at these words. Why on earth did she need money for a man? Was it a boyfriend who required assistance? Perhaps she was involved in something unsavory?

"Please meet her," Miranda pleaded. Hartley found himself agreeing. It was easier to stand up to an irate board of directors than to remain firm in front of those beseeching blue eyes.

"Tell Burnett I can't make it for dinner," he said. "I told him this morning I was hoping to take my lawyer to the club to iron out a few details of the new contract. Though perhaps it might be a good idea to delay that," he added dryly.

"Don't delay anything," Miranda said sharply. "Meet Claire first and then decide what to do."

"Very well." He caught her slender hand and held it against his cheek. "When will I see you alone, love?"

"I don't know. We have to settle this thing with Jamie first. At the moment I'd be scared for us to meet. Try to understand how I feel, Hartley."

"Alright," he sighed and dropped her hand.

"I'll see you tonight at the house," she whispered.

She quickly left the room before he had an opportunity to change his mind.

"He wants a wife? Really, Miranda! What kind of interview would I have to endure for *that* job?" Claire attempted to be funny because she could not believe she had heard her friend correctly.

"I'm serious," Miranda stated. Her nerves were beginning to fray. "I am faced with a problem and I'm counting on you to help me out."

Claire stared at Miranda, realizing that she was, indeed, deeply serious. "If Mr. Dale wants to get married so badly, I don't see why it should be *your* problem Miranda. Shouldn't that remain just his problem?"

"Well, he doesn't particularly want to get married. Therein lies the problem. Rather, he *has* to."

"Uh huh. And does he know that you are asking me to fill this vacancy?" Claire insisted. "Or is this something you've dreamed up all on your own."

"Of course he knows. Hartley isn't the kind of man you can tell what to do. We discussed it together this afternoon, at his office."

"Uh huh," Claire repeated. "And you two decided that I would be a suitable candidate?"

"No. I decided it. Hartley has agreed to meet with you, provided you're willing of course." Miranda smiled coyly.

"Not so fast!" Claire said, a little too loudly. "First of all, tell me why this highly successful, clever and, by all accounts, handsome man just hasn't been clever or successful enough to find his own lady?"

"He's been far too busy with his career."

"I'm sure he could have found someone suitable if he took a few days off from his oh-so-very busy schedule," Claire said sarcastically. "Honestly Miranda, you must be crazy to think I'd agree to such a foolish plan. I don't even know the man. From the little bit you've told me about him, I don't even like him!"

"You'd like him very much if you met him. He's coming here this evening to meet you, as a matter of fact."

"Then he'll have wasted a trip."

"Well, he's coming to see Burnett too."

"Well, good for him. Now, it won't be a wasted trip"

"Oh come on Claire," Miranda said in exasperation. "I thought you wanted to help Charles?"

"What does Charles have to do with any of this?"

"He needs forty thousand dollars, doesn't he? And Hartley will pay you fifty thousand dollars if you become his wife – with another fifty thousand dollars given to you on the day that the marriage is annulled."

Claire swayed a little. "Did you say fifty thousand dollars?"

"Yes, that's right. Fifty when you marry Hartley, and another fifty when the marriage is ended. He will only need you to be his wife for a couple of years, quite probably even less time. That's why it's important for him to choose someone who would be willing to step out of their current life and enter into this business deal. Someone who is able to put their life on hold for a time."

"My God, Miranda. This is too much to process right now." Claire did indeed look a little pale.

"Just think Claire. You could have fifty thousand dollars by this time next week," Miranda said quietly.

"Yeah, I am thinking." Claire stood up and moved around the room, her steps so light that they barely seemed to touch the carpet, her long hair swinging around her shoulders like black silk. "But why so much money? And why me? There must be some catch!"

"The money is because this is a business transaction. You – because well, you were the first person to come to mind. You would be in a position of great confidentiality with Hartley. It would be important for him to have trust in your discretion. After all, as his 'wife' you will probably hear a lot of information about the business that people would give their eye teeth to know." Miranda glanced at her fingers and thoughtfully twirled one of her large diamond rings.

"Actually I thought of you because of Charles too, Claire. Fifty thousand pounds would stop him from losing his job or getting arrested and spending time in jail."

Claire ran the pink tip of her tongue over her soft lips. "And you said Hartley would be coming here this evening?"

"Yes, later – after dinner," Miranda relaxed and sighed, knowing that she had achieved the most difficult part of what she had set out to do. To finally convince Hartley that he must use Claire as a cover would be far less difficult. "There will only be you and me for dinner tonight," she murmured. "I've persuaded Burnett to eat in his room and then afterwards we can go and sit with him until Hartley arrives."

"Until Hartley arrives to inspect me," added Claire.

"Well, yes. But I would imagine that you would be inspecting him as well. It will be equal."

"Why should he inspect me? He's the one who has to get married."

"Only out of necessity. He doesn't really want to," Miranda paused. "He loves his freedom, Claire. He wouldn't expect the marriage to tie him down."

"I couldn't care less what the hell he does with his time. I would be there when he needs me but otherwise I have my own life to live. That is, if I decide to go ahead with it. I am still not sure at this point."

Miranda lowered her eyes to hide the look of triumph glinting there. She had done it. Claire would accept the deal. There was no doubt of that. All she had to do now was to get Hartley to make the proposal.

"Well, let's just start with meeting him," she purred. She linked arms affectionately with the younger girl and guided her out of the room and down the stairs.

"Let's go eat, Claire."

Chapter 3:

Whenever Miranda invited Claire to dinner, she accepted without hesitation. It was such a pleasure to eat food that she had not prepared herself. It was even more enjoyable to eat expensive foods she considered luxuries - foods that she had only read about in gourmet magazines. Tonight's dinner was no exception.

Rich, beef consommé was followed by delicious, juicy filet mignon and roasted potato, with a side of buttery peaches-and-cream sweet corn. Dessert was fresh raspberries with homemade vanilla ice cream. Claire could see the pieces of real vanilla bean in the ice cream. She asked for a dollop of whipped cream on top of her dessert. Miranda ate sparingly, but Claire tackled her food with gusto, happily accepting a second helping of dessert.

"For such a thin little thing, you eat like a horse," Miranda commented. "Aren't you worried about getting fat?"

"Nope," Claire swallowed a last mouthful of dessert and popped a final raspberry into her mouth. She set down her spoon and licked her lips. "I don't know what you're worried about either; you're thin as a rail." She gazed at Miranda. "I wish your clothes fit me. You have no idea how my friends fight over the second-hand clothes you give me."

"You aren't any fatter than me. Just shorter. I'm sure my clothes would fit if you just had them altered."

"Probably," Claire admitted. "The real reason I don't wear them is that I wouldn't feel comfortable. They are just not my style. I'd feel like a sparrow dressed up in peacock feathers!"

Miranda laughed out loud in spite of herself. Claire always managed to put her into a good mood. It was her dry wit and her ability to make a point in the nicest possible way. Claire would do very well for Hartley. She was not dull so that she would drive him to find other female company when Miranda was not available. Nor was she sufficiently attractive to compete with Miranda and take his affections away from her. Yes, little Claire was a perfect choice.

After dinner, Miranda linked her arm through Claire's and led the way into Burnett's sitting room. Though he didn't dine with them, he had changed into a dinner jacket and was reclining in his chair, a book in his hand. He immediately put the book down as they came in. Miranda's 'doting wife act' was faultless and she kissed him on the forehead and gracefully sank into a chair beside him, acting as though she were the genuinely loving wife he believed her to be.

Watching them, Claire marveled at her friend's ability to maintain such an act for, though Miranda was too loyal to discuss her marriage to Burnett, it was evident that they only enjoyed a platonic relationship. Yet, it must have been sufficiently satisfying for Miranda to remain with him, and there was no doubt whatever that, for his part, Burnett adored his young and beautiful wife. Did Miranda ever feel that she was wasting her life by remaining with a man old enough to be father? As always, Claire dismissed the question without finding an answer.

"And how is my second favorite woman?" Burnett Farber teased Claire as he held out his hands to her.

"All the better for seeing you," she bent down to kiss him. "I read about you in the business section of the newspaper this morning."

"I thought you didn't read the financial section?"

"I always have to when I'm coming here Burnett. It gives me something to talk about with you."

"Complain about, you mean," he laughed. "Come on now, Claire, tell me what I did wrong this time.'

"Well, you didn't give a frank enough statement to the shareholders when you bought out their company."

"What are you two talking about?" Miranda asked.

"Claire is being all-knowing about a little property company I recently acquired."

"I would hardly call twenty million dollars worth of assets little," Claire murmured.

About to reply to Claire, Burnett paused listening. "I think I hear Hartley's car."

Miranda crossed to the window and pulled back the curtain. "You're right. He's just arrived."

Claire forced herself to main calm, and kept her eyes away from the door behind her as, a moment later, she heard it open and a soft spoken voice say, "Good evening." Only when the owner of the voice moved past her chair to greet his host did she get her first sight of him.

He was so big! He was a huge, dark haired bear, although he moved with such grace, as light on his feet as a boxer and with the same suggestion of controlled power. Not even his well-tailored dinner jacket could disguise his authority and sway. He was still bent over Burnett and she could not see his face, though she noticed that his hair was sleek and thick and curly. Then he straightened up and turned to be introduced to her. She saw that his face was bronze, with a strong, square jaw, pursed mouth and watchful eyes. His eyes were very dark brown, almost black.

"Good evening," he said, and his grasp of her hand was firm before he let it go and eased himself into a leather chair beside her. He spoke to Burnett, telling him what had taken place during the dinner meeting with this lawyer. She tried to listen and make sense of what he was saying but she was too conscious of his physical presence; of his height and the width of his shoulders; his strong neck and curly, shining hair – and most of all his light, soft voice that seemed in direct contrast to the masculinity he exuded. Would she have been overwhelmed under normal circumstances? Or was she feeling this way because she knew he had come here to inspect her with a view to marriage?

"I understand that you and Miranda were at university together?" Hartley turned to Claire.

He was speaking directly to her for the first time, and she gathered her wits about her and nodded. "Yes, we were."

"Did she really wear diamond jewelry to class or was that just a story she told me?"

"No, she certainly did wear her diamonds. But she'll always be remembered for wearing her fur coat to class during the winter months."

"She's always been like that," Burnett Farber chuckled. "That's my little minx. She has been on the best-dressed list every year since I married her."

"Miranda has always been very fashion conscious," Claire said. "I'd never be voted best-dressed, that's for sure."

"Why must you be so deprecating when you talk about yourself, Claire?" Burnett asked.

"Honesty isn't deprecating, Burnett. You have to be tall to look elegant. Look at all the fashion models. Most of them are close to six feet tall."

Hartley's surprise grew as he listened to this young woman talk. She was unlike anything he might have anticipated and was definitely not the type of woman he had expected to be a friend of Miranda's. But she wasn't a friend – not exactly. Hadn't Miranda said something about taking pity on her because of her circumstances?

"Perhaps you could give Claire a ride home, Hartley?" Miranda's voice roused him from his thoughts.

"Of course. I'd be happy to," he said promptly and looked at the dark-haired petite woman sitting beside him. "You don't mind if I have a few words alone with Burnett first, do you?"

He watched Claire's face as she nodded then went over to bid Burnett good night. There was an old-fashioned air about the way she bent down to embrace and kiss the older man. So, this was Miranda's choice for him? Claire Evans did not look like a girl who would cause him trouble and, as such, she might be exactly what he was looking for, provided he was going to do as Miranda wished and get married after all. He shied away from the thought. He did not want to marry anyone except Miranda.

"I'll wait downstairs for you Mr. Dale," Claire said, and he gave her an absent-minded smile before turning to Burnett.

Miranda turned to Claire as they went back to her sitting-room. "Well? Isn't he as charming as I said?"

"Are brown bears charming?" Claire smiled. "That's what he looks like to me. He's huge!"

"I must tell Hartley you see him as a bear," Miranda said with amusement.

"Don't you dare tell him that!"

"He won't mind. He has a fine sense of humor."

"No, but I will mind."

"Does that mean that you're going to consider what I asked you?" Claire gave a non-committal grunt. "*He* has to consider it too."

"Listen. Hartley needs a temporary wife," Miranda said firmly, "and you need the money. It's an ideal arrangement."

Twenty minutes later Hartley bid Burnett good night and, with a murmur, Miranda glided from the room. Left alone, Claire considered the position, her mind on Charles' predicament. Though disillusioned by what he had done, she still felt obligated to help him. His kindness to her when she had been most in need made this imperative. But until tonight – with Miranda's incredible suggestion – she had seen no way of coming to his aid. Now a kindly fate was giving her a chance to repay him. Two years of her life in exchange for Charles' good name and freedom seemed such a small price to pay. The door opened and the object of this fate stood there, his coat over his arm.

"Are you ready to go?"

Claire jumped up and he held the door open for her. She saw Miranda in the corridor and the three of them went down the stairs to the front hall.

"Call me," Miranda said softly to Hartley, and Claire saw the bear nod his head.

Miranda's concern surprised her until she remembered how much it would benefit Burnett to have a Chief Executive Director whom he trusted implicitly in charge of the company to which he had devoted most of his life. At the thought of Burnett, some of Claire's repugnance at what she was planning lessened. If marriage to Hartley Dale made Burnett more content, it would be well worth doing. It made the mercenary aspect of this arrangement easier to take. With a sigh, she took the front passenger seat of Hartley's black Mercedes.

"Where do you live?" he asked as they moved away from the Farber's home.

"Waterdown, about an hour away." The car slowed down as his foot came off the accelerator and she could not help but giggle. "But you don't have to drive me there tonight. I'm staying at a friend's house right downtown, near the Beaches."

"That's a relief." He replaced his foot on the gas pedal and they quickened speed. "We should talk about some details but do you mind if I park somewhere first? I prefer to concentrate on just one thing at a time."

"You give me the impression of being able to concentrate on many things at the same time," Claire answered.

"Part of my success lies in giving the wrong impression!" he said humorously, and then lapsed into silence until he drew the car to a stop in an empty school parking lot. Then he swiveled around and surveyed her slowly.

She stared back at him with equal candor, noticing how the moonlight turned him into a beautiful image not unlike the models she saw on the cover of men's fashion magazines. She knew the moonlight did far less for her. "I must look like a witch right now, with my pale face and black hair."

"You're younger than I expected," he said abruptly.

"I'm twenty-seven. I look younger because I'm small."

"It's more than size that makes you look young. I presume that Miranda has told you that I want a wife?"

"She told me that you *need* one; that's different, isn't it?"

"Don't play with words," he said brusquely. "Are you willing or aren't you?"

"Are *you*?"

The question took him by surprise. "I suppose I must be. If I wasn't then I wouldn't be talking to you like this. It just happened today that I – that I realized I needed to get married. It meant an entire readjustment of my thinking."

"I'm sure it did," she said carefully. "But if you want to become Chief Executive Director of Farber Investments, I assume you won't mind having to make some sacrifices."

His head tilted sharply. "I don't consider it would be a sacrifice to marry you, Ms. Evans. For your age you appear to be an eminently sensible young woman."

"How old are *you*, Mr. Dale?"

If he was startled, he didn't show it. "Thirty-four. But far older than that in experience."

"Miranda said it would be for two years," Claire murmured.

"That is merely an approximate timeline, yes."

"Will you be giving up the Chief Executive Directorship after that amount of time?"

"I certainly hope not."

"Then why will you only need a wife for two years? I'm sorry to be so curious, but I do like to get the details straight."

"And very sensible of you to do so. Let's say I only see my social life as being a problem for the next couple of years." He hesitated. "I believe Miranda has spoken to you about the financial arrangements?"

"Yes. Fifty thousand dollars on the day I marry you and fifty thousand on the day we get divorced. It's a large sum of money."

"I expect good service for it," he stated.

"What do you mean by that?"

"By service, I mean the social side of marriage only – not the physical side."

Her cheeks burned and she was angry for having asked such a question. She should have known that a man such as Hartley Dale would not need to buy sexual favors. Her curiosity stirred and the question she had asked Miranda came forcibly to mind. How could it be that a man of such obvious good looks and virility was not already married if he so desired? Somehow the excuse of no time and too much work just did not ring true.

"What is worrying you, Claire?"

His question made her realize that she had been quiet for a time. "I was just wondering why you aren't married already?"

"I have no secret vice that has prevented me from marrying," he said dryly. "So you can set your mind at rest on that."

"Then why can't you find your own woman?"

"I don't want one. I haven't even begun to think about a wife.

The necessity only arose today, and Miranda immediately suggested you. She said that you need the money as much as I need a wife. Also, she assured me that you are trustworthy and discreet and you won't mind being bought off when I no longer need you."

The brutal honesty of the words left her breathless. "You're very forthright Mr. Dale."

"I like honesty," he said and then added quickly, "whenever possible." He moved slightly and one side of his face was made silver by the moonlight. "Well, Claire Evans, are you willing to be my bride?"

"Well, I'm just overcome with emotion at that proposal," she answered coyly.

"If you marry me, you will have to change your name to Claire Dale."

"Yes, I suppose I will. Hmmm. Claire Dale. Doesn't sound too imposing. Still, I'm not a very imposing-looking person."

"You will suit me just fine."

"You're taking me on blind faith," she persisted. "I might have a terrible temper or eat my food with my fingers or burp at the dinner table."

"You went to a good university," he shrugged, "and Miranda tells me that you have acted as her social secretary from time to time. Don't minimize yourself, Claire. I dislike people who do that. Most of the time they are merely fishing for compliments."

"I'm sorry Mr. Dale. I'll try not to do that in future."

"The name is Hartley. Please call me Hartley. I think it will make the act seem more genuine," he smiled.

She laughed. "I will remember that." She looked over at him, expecting him to say more, and was disappointed when he switched on the ignition and started to drive away.

Following her directions, he drew up opposite her friend's house and switched off the ignition. "How will one week from Friday suit you Claire?"

"Suit me? For what?"

"For getting married."

"So soon?"

"There's no reason for us to wait longer, is there?"

"Oh no. The quicker I marry you, the quicker I can get..." Her voice trailed off and she was aware of him looking at her with a sign of curiosity.

"You must need this money very badly if you're willing to marry a stranger to get it," he said softly. "Miranda told me it was for a man."

"Yes, I do. I have to – if it weren't for that – I would never have agreed to your proposal or anything else remotely resembling this ...um...arrangement."

"Does it mean that much to you?"

"Yes," she said stiltedly.

Hartley leaned forward. "Are you selling yourself in order to get him?"

She caught her breath at the implication. "You mean am I getting this cash in order to get myself a boyfriend?? That's a horrid thing to say! Not to mention pre-historic. I thought dowries were a thing of the past!"

"I thought you liked frankness, Claire."

"Not when it's cruel – or unsubstantiated."

"I don't mean to be cruel. I am just curious about why you are doing this?"

"Well I don't intend to answer that question. This is a business arrangement, Hartley. Let's keep it that way."

"As you wish." He opened his door and, despite the speed with which she opened hers, was walking beside her up the steps to the front door. "There's only one other thing we have to talk about," he said. "Burnett Farber. I would like him to believe that we are getting married for the proper reasons."

She stared up at him, having to tilt her head to do so. "How can he believe that? He is a very smart man. You know that. My goodness, we've only met tonight."

"Don't you believe in love at first sight, Claire?"

"Well, you're obviously hoping that Burnett does!"

His smile indicated his appreciation of her quick reply. "I'll phone you and give you a date for lunch this week," he said. "There are a few things to discuss before we get married." He touched her arm with light but firm fingers. "Thank you for agreeing to this, Claire. I don't think either of us will regret it."

She watched him go down the steps to his car and was still standing there as he drove away. What on earth had she just agreed do? What was she in for? These were questions she would ask herself many times in the future.

And, at this moment, she had no idea of the anguish the answers would give her.

Chapter 4:

Claire met Hartley for lunch on Friday at the Four Seasons Café. It was exactly one week before the date he had arranged for their wedding. The Four Seasons was an expensive choice, and one, which made her aware of the unfashionable beige jersey dress she was wearing. But perhaps this tall, commanding-looking man was not fashion conscious. After all, if he was too busy to find his own wife, he might also be too busy to notice what she wore.

"You will need to buy some new clothes," he said, interrupting her thoughts and tearing them into mist. "I suggest you let Miranda help you."

"I won't deck myself out in gold and silver evening dresses!" she retorted.

He looked momentarily put out and then reluctantly smiled. "I thought she might be able to guide you toward the right places to go."

"Well, when you have enough money, there is never a problem to find the right places."

"Don't worry Claire. You will have more than enough money."

"I wasn't hinting," she added quickly.

"I know that. As I told you before Claire, I do appreciate your honesty. I have enough deception and pretext going on in my business life without having to resort to mincing words in my private one."

"What will I be expected to do, Hartley?" She had been thinking about asking this question all week. Looking over at him, sitting so properly, she had to admit that he made her extremely self-conscious. It must be due to his physique. He had a fearless, strong face that was at variance with his soft, gentle voice. Which aspect was indicative of the real man? There was no point in asking him and she wasn't able to look to her own heart for the answer. He was a total mystery to her.

"I'll expect you to run my home." His words forced her to

concentrate on what he was saying. She had been lost in her thoughts.

"Why? I'm sure you won't want me to do any redecorating."

"Miranda has invited us to have dinner with them tomorrow night. It would be a good idea to let Burnett know that you've been to my apartment."

She blushed, and then asked. "Do you want him to think we're already lovers?"

He looked positively nonplussed. Then he smiled. "I think my request for honesty is going to rebound! Are you always so outspoken?"

"It is my one failing." She waited to say it was a virtue, but he didn't do so. Instead, he picked up the menu and studied it. She did the same and not until they had given their order did he speak personally again. "I want Burnett to get the impression that we are seeing a great deal of each other. After all, if we're going to get married in one week's time…"

"When are you going to tell him?"

"Some time next week."

"Why can't he know the truth about our arrangement?"

"No one must know. Don't question me about it, Claire. Just take my word for it."

"I have no intention of questioning you," she said calmly. "I'm not sufficiently interested in your private affairs."

He stared at her.

"May I remind you that our arrangement is a business one?" she cooed.

Melon and prosciutto was set before them and she picked up her spoon and fork and began to eat. "This is so cool!" she murmured. "I love melon."

"Oh good. They do a really *kewl* rice pudding too!" he mimicked.

She glared at him from beneath her lashes but decided to ignore the remark.

After lunch they drove to Hartley's condominium, an opulently furnished apartment near Lakeshore Drive at the Harbourfront, beside the ferry docks. It was at the top floor – penthouse level – with a terrace on two sides that gave them a wonderful view of the lake. The furniture was imported Italian, mostly leather and very dark. There were only one or two pictures on the walls.

"You aren't very interested in your home, are you?" she commented.

He shrugged. "It's somewhere to sleep."

"It will have to be more than that if we are supposed to do social entertaining."

"Social entertaining?"

"Isn't that why you're getting married?"

He nodded quickly. "If you wish to make any alterations, by all means do so."

"Would you like me to ask Miranda first?"

"Don't be sarcastic with me, Claire."

"I wasn't being sarcastic," she said truthfully. "I have my own ideas when it comes to clothes, but I don't know anything about home decorating."

"I'm sure you can manage on your own. Don't ask Miranda."

"I would only want to alter a few things," she said, looking around. "I'd like some fabric-covered chairs and a bit more color in this room. Needs some plants and flowers. It's a little dull."

"For a girl who favors beige jersey..." he began.

"Just wait until you see me in the very expensive new clothing I intend to buy with all your money!"

He laughed. "I'm glad you aren't shy to talk about money." He stopped as though he was about to say more, then stopped and glanced at his watch. Taking the hint, she walked to the door ahead of him and he followed her to the elevator.

"I'll pick you up tomorrow night," he said suddenly. "It will look better if we arrive at the Farber's together."

The last part of his sentence took away the pleasure from the first part. She was surprised with herself for noticing it. Hartley had made it quite clear that their relationship was a business one, and it was silly of her to regard it differently.

Yet, despite reminding herself that she was marrying him solely in order to help Charles, she could not restrain a thrill of anticipation as she waited for him to pick her up the following evening. Knowing that she would be receiving a clothing allowance from him, she dipped into her savings and bought a new dinner dress. It was a flowing silk dress with a delicate floral pattern. It could have been a track suit for all the comment it drew from him as he came towards her. She quickly put her coat around her shoulders and became angry at herself for being hurt by his disinterest.

He looked even more handsome that she remembered. He was again wearing a dinner jacket, though this one was not black but slate gray with slender black pinstripes on it. It made his hair look even darker and more luxurious. He had driven a jade green Jaguar this time. She was glad that the car was warm because the dress, though lovely, was lightweight and a little cool for the November weather.

"You should buy a couple of furs," he commented as though reading her thoughts.

"Furs! I don't think so. I would prefer wool, or velvet or fake fur."

"Mink," he replied. "Or perhaps ermine. Mink might be too much for your stature. Seal would do nicely too."

"Though I would never wear a dead animal on my person, I must say you sure seem knowledgeable about furs," she commented.

"Well we made a take-over bid for a fur company last year, and I always make it my business to know as much as I can about any company we buy."

"I will find something just as nice as real fur. You can trust me on that."

"Well, ultimately it is your choice Claire."

She turned in her seat and looked at him. "What did you do before you worked for Burnett Farber?"

"I lectured in Economics at the University of British Columbia for a few years. At the end of my illustrious career there, I became president of the university and a member of many boards of trade."

"At your young age? You're kidding!"

"Most people are surprised to hear about my background," he conceded, "Not because of my past, but because I've been such a success in the business world. Mind you, I am a graduate of the Harvard Business School too. I suppose that helps."

Claire laughed. "Yeah, that would help just a little bit. How could you stand to give up academic life for the rat race?"

"Because these rats live better!"

"So you sold your soul for money?"

"Well, you're doing the same."

She went red and tried to gain control. "Only for two years, Mr. Dale."

"Call me darling," he teased. "And don't forget to smile at me lovingly tonight."

"Oh don't worry darling. I'll kill you with love!"

He chuckled. "I bet you would too."

Still amused by her comment, they arrived at the Farber home and he parked the car beside Burnett's Rolls Royce. They entered the marble hall and climbed the stairs to the drawing-room. There were several guests already present and Burnett, giving no indication that he had a bad heart, was chatting with a group of men as they came in.

"How lovely that you were able to come," he greeted Claire, and she was aware of him looking at her with faint surprise, as if he couldn't understand why Hartley had chosen to bring her as his dinner guest.

Occasionally throughout the evening she saw him glance over with a puzzled look, though now she knew it was due to Hartley's behavior towards her. It could by no means be called overt – he was far too careful for that – but the way he remained by her side and allowed his hand to rest on her arm was considerably more than casual. Even knowing it to be an act did not stop her from feeling desirable because of his attentions. The other women in the room were casting envious glances at her and she was well aware of it. She wondered if Hartley felt she compared well with them and tried to gain some comfort from her new dress. But against Miranda's superbly cut burgundy velvet gown, it looked dull and ordinary, and she could see why Hartley had not commented on her appearance when he had picked her up. In a country pond, she might be the goldfish, but in the big city pool, she was just a minnow.

"Wake up sleepyhead," Hartley's voice was soft in her ear as he bent over her chair.

"Forgive me," she apologized, quickly lifting her lids and blinking, "but I was up at five o'clock this morning." She couldn't believe she had fallen asleep.

"Why?"

"I had signed on for an early morning shift with the Distress Centre hotline. Plus I was up late last night to make last minute plans for a spiritual retreat we're holding in Waterdown."

"Well, no wonder you feel tired." He hoisted her gently to her feet, keeping one hand in his as they walked over to say good night to Miranda and Burnett.

"I hear it's all settled," Miranda whispered as Claire drew close.

"Yes. We're getting married next Friday."

"I know. I haven't told Burnett yet because Hartley thought it would be better not to make it look so rushed. Have you told your cousin about the money?"

Claire nodded, aware of Hartley standing next to her and not sure whether he could hear what was being said.

"Charles must have been very pleased," Miranda insisted.

"Very," Claire said stiffly and was glad was Hartley moved towards to door to leave.

"Who is Charles?" he asked as they drove away.

"You heard that?"

"I can lip-read."

"I'd better watch out for you, then."

"Answer me, Claire."

"I thought our personal lives were our own."

"From next Friday onwards you will share your personal life with me. It will remain that way for as long as we're married."

"Really? Well, that cuts both ways, *darling*."

He caught his breath for a moment but when he spoke again his voice was as calm as before. "I have no personal life. Now then, is Charles the man for whom you need the money?"

"Yes."

"Why does he require it?"

"For business reasons."

"I see."

She knew that he didn't, and waited nervously for his next question. But when it came, it surprised her.

"You must care a great deal for this Charles if you're marrying me in order to give him fifty thousand dollars."

"Actually, all he needs is forty thousand. But that was the amount that Miranda quoted so I didn't negotiate."

"Are you going to answer my question?"

"What was that again?"

"I asked," he began patiently, "if you care a great deal for Charles."

"Yes, I do care for him. We grew up together. He's my third cousin."

"You're very close for him to be your third cousin."

"Well, we grew up together," she repeated. "I look on him as a brother."

"You're certainly a loving sister to be giving him so much money. But you still haven't told me why he needs it so badly."

Ashamed to tell the truth, she said the first thing that came into her head. "I *want* him to have it. I would do anything for Charles. He means more to me than anyone else in this world."

"I see." They drove in silence for awhile before he spoke again. "There's no need to get upset, Claire. I merely wanted to establish what your relationship was with this man. Now that I know, the subject is closed."

"He isn't in love with me, if that's what you're getting at." This was one thing she was determined to make clear.

"That is obvious. You wouldn't be giving him all that money if he was."

She turned on him, furious. "I am *not* buying his affection. If he doesn't get that money, he'll....He needs it in order to expand his business."

"Are you sure that he'll wait two years for you?"

She clenched her hands and resolutely refused to answer him. If Hartley persisted in misunderstanding her, she was not going to quarrel with him about it. They completed the drive to her destination in silence and, as he had done on the first night, he escorted her to her door.

"We have a few more things to talk over before we get married," Hartley said. "I think that…"

"If you've changed your mind because of Charles, I understand," she interrupted.

"I haven't changed my mind!" He gave her a little shake, grasping her at the shoulders. "You silly girl. You can do what you like with the money I give you. I'm only concerned that you don't make a fool of yourself. I'd have thought you would like to spend some of that money on yourself or your house in Waterdown. Or do you intend on selling it?"

"Of course not! That house is the only thing I have. I mean at the end of …I mean when the marriage is over, I'll go back to my home."

"Perhaps we can go there for the odd weekend, if you like," he said gently. "I've always wanted a place in the country."

"Why when you already have a large house plus a lakefront condominium?"

"It doesn't suit my life right now. A home in the country is for married men, with children."

She sensed a sadness in his voice and longed to tell him she would try to give him the companionship that he seemed to yearn for. But unexpected shyness kept her silent and she merely gave him her hand and said good night.

"Don't forget that you're spending this weekend with me at

THE HIRED BRIDE

Jackson's Point," he reminded her. "The Robertsons asked me to bring you."

"Was that the thin couple Burnett was talking to for such a long time?"

"Yes. Robertson is chairman of a small company we are interested in buying. This weekend will be an excuse for us to have a little exploratory chat."

"Do you ever do anything purely for fun?"

"Of course I do." He seemed taken aback. There was a slight pause. "I *am* human, you know."

"Yes," Claire said quietly. "You certainly are." She wished that she could have met him under normal circumstances. That would have been exciting. A man of such good looks, smarts and personality had never come into her life before.

But then, there were not many men like Hartley Dale – thank goodness for that – for if there were many tears would be shed and hearts broken.

"What deep thoughts are going on behind that head of yours?" he asked, and she flashed him such a brilliant smile that he was suddenly aware of just how pretty she was. She just didn't smile that often. Her hair was dark and glossy. With those inquiring eyes, she reminded him of a raven.

"What are *your* deep thoughts?" she countered.

"I asked you that question first, you naughty girl! But just to show you how magnanimous I am, I'll admit that I was thinking you looked like a glossy black raven just now."

"What?" she said, with irony. "You couldn't go along with popular opinion and see me as a little mouse?"

"I've paid you a compliment, Claire." He said firmly. "Birds are lovely creatures, delicate, smart and full of interest, provided you have the patience to watch them. But now that I've answered your question, you have to answer mine."

"I've forgotten what I was thinking, actually…"

"I had the impression that you were coming to some deduction about me and I was curious to know what it was."

She hesitated and then decided to be truthful. In a situation like this, honesty was the only true thing they could offer each other. "I was thinking what a good thing it was that you have been so preoccupied with your work. Otherwise, you would have gone around breaking many hearts."

"I haven't been celibate," he said abruptly. "Don't let Miranda kid you that I am."

"She hasn't spoken of you in detail to me. Not really."

"Well, that's a relief. When two women sit down to dissect a man, they don't leave much of him whole."

"Don't generalize, Hartley!" she chided him. "You speak like a frightened male. I never thought you would care at all what anybody said about you."

"I don't."

"Well, then you're invincible in that armor," she murmured, and heard him catch his breath. His next words were a complete change of subject.

"I'm going to pick you up this Friday evening between four and five." He eyed her up and down. "The women generally dress for dinner, but other than that it will be casual during the day."

"I do know how the rich live," she replied. "I've been around Miranda for a few years now."

"No offence meant, Miss Jump-down-my-Throat!"

"None taken, darling," she laughed. She waved goodbye and walked into her friend's apartment building, waiting in the foyer until he drove away. Again she found herself wishing that she had been given the opportunity to meet this handsome man under normal circumstances. Yet, she would probably never have met him, for their social orbits were too different. It was incredible to think that she would be spending the next couple of years as his wife, pretending they had a normal marriage. It was a frightening thought, and only the knowledge that, by doing it she was helping Charles, prevented her from immediately changing her mind.

"I must be suffering from the pre-wedding jitters," she whispered and then laughed. Having the chance of receiving a sum of money that would have taken her five or six years to earn, she would be crazy to turn this opportunity down.

Upstairs in her friend's apartment, she noticed that no one was home. Gillian had left a note saying she was staying over at her boyfriend's place. She went into the guest room and surveyed the new silk dress as she took it off and hung it in the closet.

Hartley had not liked it. His lack of comment had been indicative of that. If it had met with his approval, he would have said so. She took out the dress again and held it in front of herself in the full-length mirror behind the door. She had spent far more on it than she normally did, but in comparison with the dresses worn at the party tonight, this one was cheap-looking. Now depressed, she flung it on to a chair and got into bed. Trousers of tweed and black wool would probably be required for the weekend, along with sweaters of expensive cotton or cashmere. She would need a couple of long dresses for the evenings. Hartley made that perfectly clear. Well, he was going to be in for a surprise if he thought her wardrobe would cover that. The only long dress she possessed was the new one. As for tweeds and wool trousers? She smiled as she considered her one navy blue suit and the four pairs of jeans she owned - that plus a couple of track pants and sweatshirts. Not that she normally cared about her appearance, but she wanted to look sufficiently glamorous to make him look at her with appreciation. Well, any male eyes would be nice, she told herself, not just one pair in particular.

Claire overslept in the morning, a luxury she rarely allowed herself. But she was staying in Toronto to do some work for Miranda, who was giving a large dinner party during the weekend and wished her to arrange the menu and all the catering for it. This thought made her realize that Burnett and Miranda would not be at the Robertson's during the weekend. It was unnerving to think this would be the first time she would be alone with Hartley. Still, it was something she had to get used to, for once she was his wife there would be many such times. She would even get used to being alone with him without

the benefit of casual friends around.
There was a knock at the door.
"Yes?" Claire called out.
"It's the landlady. Is Gillian here?"
Claire got up and wrapped a robe around her. She went to the door and opened it. There stood Gillian's landlady with curlers in her hair and an envelope in her hand. Claire couldn't remember the woman's name.
"Hello dear, are you staying for a couple of days?"
"Yes, just until Friday morning. Hope you don't mind."
"Not at all, Claire. Listen, an envelope arrived by courier just now. It's addressed to you. They didn't know who else to buzz so they just pressed the button marked "Super"."
Claire took the envelope out of the woman's hands. "Oh thanks so much. I hope they didn't disturb you."
"Not at all, lovey. It happens all the time."
Surprised, Claire looked at the envelope. The writing was heavy and bold and instinctively she knew it was Hartley's. With shaking fingers, she opened the envelope and took out a single sheet of thick notepaper. Something fluttered to the floor and, picking it up, she saw that it was a cheque for five thousand dollars. With heart hammering, she read the letter.
"After I left you last night," he wrote, "I realized that you might be short of cash. When you are my wife I will expect you to dress accordingly, so I hope you don't mind if I jump the gun by a few days and give you a cheque today. If it isn't enough, don't hesitate to let me know. We will have to discuss a clothing allowance for you when we meet. In the meantime, enjoy yourself with this." Then his signature, simply written, was at the bottom without any of the flourishes she had expected.
She folded the letter and put it together with the cheque into her handbag. If all the money she had spent on clothes in the past five years were added up, she doubted if it would amount to the sum Hartley had sent her. This, more than anything else that had yet happened, showed her how different their lifestyles were. Somehow

it boded ill for their future, and she wondered if it would be better to tell Hartley that she changed her mind and was not going ahead with the plan to marry him.

Yet the reasons for which she had accepted his proposition were as important today as they had been a week ago. She decided to say nothing. It would have been nice to be able return the cheque and say she didn't need it, but it would have been foolhardy. Claire was nothing if not practical. Too practical she thought, for men seemed to prefer women who were foolish and illogical rather than those who were confident and knew where they were going.

Small town life wasn't conducive to excitement. It was a pity she had listened to Charles and stayed in the old house. But he enjoyed the occasional weekend visits in Waterdown so much that she didn't have the heart to sell it and move to the city. Nor did she choose to rent it out and accept Miranda's offer of living in the Farber's large house and working full-time as her social secretary. Not that she regretted that decision. She admired Miranda, but she was not blind to her selfishness and she knew that, although her friend was nice enough to work for on a part-time basis, she would be far too demanding as a full-time employer.

She walked out of the apartment building and decided not to wait for the bus. She was intensely aware of the cheque in her handbag and toyed with the idea of using it right away. But there were other things more important that had to be done first. She had to speak with Charles. Claire had already told him there was a possibility of getting the forty thousand dollars he needed, and he had been so speechless with relief that he hadn't even questioned as to where or how she got the funds. His questions would come sooner or later and, deciding to make it sooner, she went into a phone booth and called him at work. Charles said he was free and they arranged on a time and place for a meeting.

An hour later, they sat opposite one another in a coffee shop, directly across the street from the company where he worked. She carefully explained her reasons for agreeing to get married to Hartley Dale.

"You're out of your mind!" Charles exploded when she had finished. "I know I'm desperate for the money, but I can't let you sacrifice your life in order to get it for me. That man must be a maniac!"

"No, he's not. Don't be silly," she protested. "He's a much respected businessman in this city."

"He might be just the opposite in his private life. Claire, you don't know what you might be getting yourself into."

"I won't be sharing his private life, at least not in the way you think. There's nothing sexual about this relationship. That much has been made clear. I will be acting as his hostess and taking care of his home."

"Couldn't he hire a housekeeper for that?"

"You can't take a housekeeper with you when you travel. You can't let a housekeeper entertain your guests."

"I still think it's very strange that he can't find a wife in the usual way."

"Perhaps it's because he doesn't want a normal kind of marriage. Charles, I get the impression that he doesn't believe in love. He's only marrying because he has to do it."

"When is the wedding?"

"One week from this Friday," Claire answered quietly.

"I don't like it," Charles said again. "I won't let you do it."

"You can't stop me! I've already given my word and I don't intend to break it."

"Does he know why you've agreed to such a crazy plan?" Charles asked.

"I've told him that I want the money to help a cousin of mine. I haven't said why you need it and Hartley assumed that I …" She stopped, too embarrassed to explain Hartley's conclusions of having to buy a man's affections. Charles' face darkened and Claire quickly added, "I didn't say anything about you borrowing company money. Hartley thinks….well, he thinks I'm using the money to buy your love."

"My *what*?"

"He thinks I'm in love with you and that if I had money, sort of like an old-fashioned dowry I presume - then I would be able to attract you."

This last statement was so bizarre that she burst out laughing. Charles stared at her in astonishment but then he slowly started to smile too. Soon, he was serious again.

"I don't really find it that funny, Claire. I know I said that I would do anything to return the loan I borrowed but I didn't mean for you to take it literally."

"I couldn't handle it if you went to prison, Charles. You're my only family. I'd be lost without you. That's probably what would happen if the company found out."

"I still can't let you…"

"Well, it's too late." She looked at him and held his hand. "Charles please, it's the only way I can repay you for all the kindness and love you're shown to me. The way you looked after me when Daddy died."

"I did no more for you than a brother would have done," he said gravely. "That's how I see you Claire - as my kid sister." He squeezed her hand. "Not such a kid anymore, I guess. I just can't imagine you as a married woman."

"I won't be – except by name."

He looked at her face and flushed, taken aback. "My God, I wasn't even thinking about the sexual side of it. Too much for me. What sort of man can Dale be to want to tie himself to someone he doesn't love?"

"I've told you. It's a business contract for a couple of years."

Charles frowned, his eyebrows meeting above his nose. He was similar in looks to Claire, though considerably taller. His jaw line was stronger and there was less of a sparkle in his eyes, but looking at them together, it was easy to see the blood relationship between them. "Just how does Mr. Dale plan to organize his social life once the two-year contract is up?"

"I asked him that same question. He really didn't have an answer for me."

"Do you think he has a permanent relationship in mind, eventually?" Charles demanded.

"I really don't think so." Claire smiled. "If pressed, I don't even think he could describe me in detail. He probably pays more attention to his own secretary."

"He'd better keep it that way. If he does anything objectionable, you let me know at once!"

"Oh sure!" Claire howled. "I can see the headlines now. 'Cousin rushes in to defend young bride from husband's sexual advances.' Honestly, you talk as if I'm still a child."

"You always will be a kid to me." Charles' frown remained. "If only we weren't having our books audited so soon. I would have been able to put the money back before anyone noticed. You do believe that I didn't mean to steal it, don't you Claire?" he asked, and then went on without waiting for her to answer. "If the bottom hadn't dropped out of the damn stock market, I would have tripled that amount within a month! As it is, the shares I bought aren't even worth one quarter of what I paid for them."

"I'll give you Hartley's cheque the minute I get it."

"I'll give you the shares in return."

"I don't want them."

"Maybe not but you're going to have them. You're paying a high price for them Claire. Two years of your life is a lot to give up."

"I would do much more than that if I had to."

"I believe that you would, Pumpkin."

Arm in arm they left the café. Claire was so engrossed with Charles that she did not notice the black car slowly moving along the street, nor Hartley Dale's startled exclamation when he saw her.

So, there is the man that Claire Evans loves, he thought, watching her every move. "I hope he isn't planning on sharing her once she's married to me," he muttered softly.

Hartley raked a hand through his hair. He didn't know whether or not he was doing the right thing in staying with Farber Investments International. Perhaps he should just resign and take his chance of eventually being able to persuade Miranda to come with him and leave Burnett. Yet she always had Burnett's ill health as her trump card, using it to frighten him into maintaining their discretion. Even yesterday, when he had seen her for an hour and pleaded with her not to let him go on with this farce of a marriage, she insisted that they were doing the only possible thing in the circumstances.

"Burnett is getting worse, not better," she had cried. "Neither of us would sleep at night if we did anything to give him a fatal heart attack. I could never forgive myself."

"Then at least agree with me that it would be better if I left and went with another firm."

"And play right into Jamie's hands? That's exactly what he wants you to do! Leave the company so that he can step into your shoes."

"Well, they're far too big for him," Hartley had retorted.

"It wouldn't stop him from trying to walk in them!"

It was this conversation, more than anything else, which had finally made Hartley agree to go on with the plan. What a surprise to learn that the sight of Claire looking adoringly up at the man she loved had unexpectedly soured him. What a strange reaction, indeed!

Still, a week from Friday he was buying all of her time and he would make damned sure she gave him all of it.

Chapter 5:

Hartley's Jaguar ate up the distance to the Robertson's house in Jackson's Point. For most of the journey Claire sat quietly, nervous of the weekend that lay ahead of her and even more nervous of the man beside her, who was driving with the ferocity of a tiger. Something must have happened to annoy him, for her had barely spoken to her since he picked her up.

"Have you been busy in the last few days?" she asked when she could no longer stand the silence.

"No more than usual."

"Have you heard some bad news?"

"No. Why do you ask?"

"Because you're driving like a demon."

"What?" The car swerved and he straightened it immediately. "What do you mean?"

"Tense at the wheel, foot hard on the accelerator. Don't you think you'd find the drive more relaxing if you just did seventy instead of ninety miles per hour?"

Instantly, he slowed down. "Don't you like going fast, Claire?"

"It wasn't the speed of the car I was thinking about, as much as the way you're *burning* yourself up!"

He chuckled and his hands – his large, long fingered hands – gripped the wheel less tautly. "You never fail to surprise me Claire."

"Well, that's good then. I wouldn't want you to become bored with me."

He mumbled his agreement and didn't speak for several moments.

"I saw you in the street the other day," he said finally. "You were with a man."

Surprised, she turned her head and looked at him. "It was Charles, the cousin I told you about."

"The man for whom you are marrying me." He made it a comment, not a question, and so she did not answer him. "Claire, if you don't want to go ahead with the marriage, you only have to say so."

"Does that mean that you've changed your mind?"

"No," he said abruptly. "I'm still prepared to go ahead with it."

She longed for him to be more explicit as to his reasons because she found it hard to believe that Burnett had only made Hartley his Chief Executive Director on condition that he take a wife. It seemed a little old-fashioned, even for Burnett. They may have made arrangements like that in the 1930's or even the 1940's but not in this day and age. Yet she could see no reason why Miranda or Hartley should have lied about it. Perhaps there were other business reasons that they did not wish to disclose. With a start, she realized that Hartley was speaking to her again and, at her look of inquiry, he repeated his question.

"I asked you to tell me something about yourself, Claire. I don't know anything beyond the fact that you went to the same university as Miranda."

"We only took the same two classes for a year," she said. "Miranda is older than I am, but we kept in touch."

"Why? You two are totally different."

"I don't really know why. Well, I know why I kept in touch with her. She was the most glamorous person I had ever met. I have no idea why she bothered with me."

"That shows what a poor judge of character you have," he teased. "Don't you know that everyone loves to have a sycophant kneeling at their feet?"

Claire snorted. "I'm no sycophant, Hartley. Believe me when I tell you that I know all of Miranda's faults."

"Tell me."

"Nope. I wouldn't dream of talking about a friend behind her back."

He grinned, but didn't tell her that Miranda would have no such qualm about gossip. *My pet lamb* was what Miranda always called Claire. He had a strange feeling that Miranda was not only doing Claire a grave injustice but showing her own lack of judgment. Claire was certainly not a lamb by nature – calling her a wolf cub might be closer to hitting the mark.

"What have I said that's so funny?" she asked, her voice full of suspicion.

"Nothing."

"Then why are you grinning? I've noticed that you do that a lot when I'm talking to you."

He thought the comment over. "I think you should be pleased by that. Not many women make me smile, Claire."

She was still thinking about this when they drew up in the curved drive that fronted a small, beautifully maintained Queen Anne house.

The Robertsons in their own home were considerably more relaxed than the couple she had met at Miranda's dinner party. Claire immediately felt at ease with them. Her hostess showed her to her room, which was well appointed with a couple of the latest best-selling novels on her bedside table, and a large ensuite bathroom all to herself.

"My husband and I will be in the sun room downstairs. When you're ready to come down, please join us there," Mrs. Robertson said. "You and Hartley are our only guests this weekend, so it's going to be informal."

"I'll enjoy that much more," Claire replied. "I was dreading a dressed-up weekend."

"It would have been that way if Miranda had been here," Mrs. Robertson turned abruptly, as if she had said more than she intended, and then with a smile went out.

Claire was not surprised by the remark, for Miranda was so lovely that she usually caused antagonism among other women. Oddly enough, she herself had never been jealous of her, nor of any other female friends. Perhaps it was because their social lives had never touched. Or perhaps the things that Miranda considered amusing, Claire found extremely boring. As Hartley's wife, she would have to condition herself to the same life as Miranda. It was a terrifying thought. For now, she refused to think about it.

She started to unpack, checking over her wardrobe carefully. If Hartley didn't like the clothes she had bought with his money, then he would just have to do the shopping himself. She giggled at the thought.

Looking at herself in the mirror before she went downstairs, she found it hard to believe that he would object to her appearance. Anticipating that the house would be cold, she had gone for warmth as well as style. The ruby velvet dress she wore had both. It had a tight bodice, which showed cleavage – rare for her; it hugged her slender waist snugly and had long, tight-fitted sleeves, showing off her lovely figure. It was slightly medieval in style, and the red color went well with her glossy black hair. Excitement gave color to her cheeks and heightened the creamy color of her skin, making her eyes glow like pools in the forest, grey and bottomless.

There was a soft knock at the door and she called, "Come in," but her racing pulse told her it was Hartley even before she saw his tall, broad-shouldered figure in the doorway.

"I came to see if you were comfortable."

"Very," she said. "It's a beautiful room. Where is yours?"

"Next door." There was a playful glint in his eye. "The Robertsons are nothing, if not diplomatic!"

"Hmmm. It would have been more diplomatic to have put us on opposite sides of the house."

"Surely not!" he protested. "Stubbing one's toes along the dark hallway in the middle of the night as we attempt to sneak into each other's room," he teased her.

Claire knew he was only joking but she could not help the swift blush that flamed her face. She turned abruptly towards the dressing table and made a pretense of searching for her brush.

"You're very innocent, aren't you?" He was close behind her, and his hands came out and pulled her back towards him, forcing her to stare into the mirror and see them standing together. She looked like a miniature beside him and felt much smaller.

"I could just put you in my pocket," he whispered and then, catching himself, released her. "Come along, Claire. You look as if you could use a drink."

There was a gentle, relaxed tone to the evening. In the small town where she lived, Claire was used to being regarded as the efficient Miss Evans, who was part-time social secretary to some rich people in Toronto and part-time social worker to the old people in town. If anyone was in trouble, if an extra pair of hands was needed or advice sought, it was always to Claire that people turned. Even the minister thought she had a better understanding of the church parishioners than he did. They had laughed about it one day at tea.

Perhaps it was only her doctor who saw her as she really was: an intelligent and resourceful young woman whose mind was barely utilized. Yet here, among these rich and sophisticated people, she was still regarded as a child. It was an attitude encouraged by her diminutiveness, and she wished that she could add six more inches to her height and an extra twenty pounds to her weight.

She sighed and leaned back against her armchair, enjoying the warmth of the fire and the pattern that the flames made upon the ceiling. Hartley sat beside her, talking quietly to John Robertson. The firelight made his hair look more lustrous and she had the feeling that she was seeing him more relaxed than he had been in a long time. He had a handsome, classic face. Age would not diminish his stature nor lessen the breadth of his shoulders, though she hoped that it might soften the determination of his chin and the hard line of his mouth. He looked like a man who had fought hard in order to achieve his ambitions and who had even greater ambitions to achieve. She shifted her head to watch him more easily. He was a man who had not yet obtained what he wanted from life and he would not rest until he had done so.

Without warning, he turned his head and caught her watching him. She found his eyes probing hers. Quickly she lowered her lids and pretended to be dozing.

"I think Claire has gone to sleep on us," Claire Robertson whispered.

"No, I haven't," Claire said clearly. "I'm wide awake and thinking."

"About the economic situation, no doubt," Hartley said dryly.

"How did you guess?"

"From your pained expression," He was still teasing. "Tell me what solutions you have for the rocking economy?"

Sitting up straight, her hands clasped on her lap, Claire proceeded to do so. Her audience could not hide their astonishment and, seeing it, she grew more reckless than she might otherwise have been, and put forward theories she would normally never have aired.

"Well, well," John Robertson gasped when she finally stopped. "If you ever want a job, let me know."

"Where did you attend university?" his wife asked.

"I went to York," Claire waited for Hartley to say something, but he remained silent and she hid her disappointment, admitting to herself that she had shown off mainly to surprise him and to make him see her as a woman and not a child.

"How about a nightcap before we go to bed?" her host asked, pouring out a couple of brandies as he spoke.

"Not for me," his wife said, and looked at Claire. "What will you have?"

"A glass of milk," Hartley spoke before Claire could do so.

"Chocolate, actually," Claire said in her gentlest tone, "and a teething ring to chew on at the same time." She looked over a Hartley. "It will save me from biting you!"

He burst out laughing and the Robertsons joined in.

"Would you really like some milk?" Mrs. Robertson asked.

"Yes," Claire stood up. "But I'll get it for myself. Please don't bother. I'm very handy in the kitchen."

Mrs. Robertson nodded at her to do as she liked, and Claire left the sitting room and crossed the hall to the kitchen. The couple who served the household had already gone to bed. She opened the refrigerator for some milk and got the cocoa out of the pantry. She was pouring the milk into a cup when she became aware of being watched and looked up to see Hartley leaning against the edge of the table.

"The Robertsons have gone to bed. They told me to say good night to you."

"Already? That was sudden. Are you going to bed too?"

"No. I'll wait for you." He held open the kitchen door and followed her back into the sitting room where he resumed his seat, his hand still clasped around the brandy snifter. "I hope you didn't mind me teasing you tonight Claire."

"I don't mind being teased sometimes. I can take it."

"And the rest of the time?"

"I prefer to be treated as an adult."

"Since you're going to be my wife next Friday, I would have thought that scolding unjustified," he said curtly.

"You give me the impression that you see me as a child, Hartley."

"You look like one."

Irritably she set her cup on the table with a clunk and turned to him. As she did so, the side of her body was outlined in the firelight, the material across her bodice strained across her breasts, pushing her cleavage up.

"Well, not quite a child," her murmured as his gaze rested on her creamy white skin. "The more I look at you, the more of a woman you become."

"Don't patronize me," she said angrily, and jumped up.

"Sit down and don't lose your temper!" Hartley spoke quietly, but firmly and she sensed the command behind the words. "Why didn't you tell me you had a degree in economics?" he asked unexpectedly.

"You didn't ask me."

"I assumed that you would tell me important aspects of your life."

"You hired me to be your wife for a couple of years, not to join your statistical department. I don't see what my degree has to do with anything."

"Now you're treating *me* like a child, Claire. You know very well what I mean. Ever since I met you, you've pretended that you have hibernated in a little town and that you worked for Miranda to earn a little fun money."

"I've done no such thing! I made it very clear to you that I need to work in order to earn a living. Why else do you think I'm marrying you?"

"To get fifty thousand dollars to give to your cousin, though why the hell you would want to do that, I cannot imagine!"

"I love Charles and I'm ..." she hesitated, wishing she could be truthful and tell him the whole story. Charles would be furious if she did.

"And you're hoping that he will feel grateful enough to do .... Do what? ...if you let him set up his own business? You're not a stupid woman Claire. You have an economics degree and you're intelligent enough to know the facts of life. Why throw yourself away on someone like Charles? What hold does he have on you? You give him this money, and what does he give you? I just don't understand!"

"You are doing your best to talk me out of marrying you, aren't you?" she said. "Is that what you want? – to back out of this thing?"

"Of course not."

She was warmed by the enthusiasm of his answer, though it faded as he added: "If you backed out, I wouldn't even bother to look for another candidate. I would simply forget the whole thing and leave the company."

She drew in a deep breath. "I still find it very hard to believe that Burnett is so insistent on you being married."

"Well, it happens to be true but, for heaven's sake, don't go talking to him about it, do you hear?"

"I wouldn't dream of discussing our little arrangement with anyone, especially not Burnett. Why would I do myself out of one hundred thousand dollars?"

"Fifty thousand," he corrected. "You won't get the other half until our marriage is annulled."

"No fear of that. Or are you afraid that I'll try to stay married to you?"

His mouth curved into a sneer. "What will you do with the second half of the money? Will you give that to poor old Charles too?"

"That's my business Mr. Dale!" She stood up again and this time he didn't try to stop her. Instead he came with her to the door.

"I'll come upstairs with you," he said tenderly. She was intensely aware that everyone in the house was asleep and she was alone with a tall, strong man who could overpower her in a moment. She was also aware of his hand on her elbow guiding her up the stairs.

"Just think of it," he said quietly. "On Friday, you will become Claire Dale."

She repeated the name and as she did so, she became aware that the tender look in his face had been replaced with a hard look. It was as if he was thinking of something unpleasant. "I'm sure there are many women who would love to be Mrs. Hartley Dale," she said quickly, hoping to restore his good humor.

"You would think so," he said with a ruthless sneer to his mouth. "Damn it, Claire, what does it matter how many there are, if it isn't the right woman!"

She longed to ask him what he meant but she knew it was unwise to do so. Besides, she had sufficient intelligence to guess that he had obviously been in love and something had gone wrong. She had never believed that he reached the age of thirty-four without being seriously in love, despite his assurance to the contrary. She wondered who the woman was and why she had not wanted him. That must be a rare person indeed to have turned down Hartley Dale. She would never do such a thing if she had the chance.

She stumbled on the stairs and would have fallen had he not put out a hand to steady her. She gripped the banister, more to stop her hand from trembling than because she needed the support. What on earth had made her think such a thing? She hardly knew anything about Hartley and the little she did know, she despised. She had always been disapproving of corporate big business and those who made their living from it, yet here she was allowing herself to be swayed by the handsome magnetism of one of the city's most successful men.

Magnetism. That was it - the magnetism of a virile, confidant man; a charisma that had nothing to do with reality. Like a silly school girl dreaming of Prince Charming, she had let herself be carried away by the tall, dark and handsome looks and the powerful physique. A relationship needed more than looks to make it meaningful, and it would auger well for her to remember this fact in the months to come. But, it wouldn't be easy.

"Are you alright? Were you dizzy?" he asked, concerned.

She felt the warm of his hands on her tiny shoulders. Large, gentle hands. She looked up at him, his dark eyes so gorgeous. She felt she could fall into those chocolate pools.

"I'm....yes...I'm fine. I must be tired," she said, haltingly.

They reached the top of the stairs, and walked along the corridor to her room.

"Good night Claire," he said and leaned down to kiss her forehead. Their eyes met. All at once, he lifted her chin and kissed her softly on the lips. The kiss felt so natural and so right. She shivered with excitement.

"Be ready for a walk with me in the morning. I'll be banging on your door at nine-thirty if you aren't downstairs by then." He smiled at her and paused.

"Sleep well, angel," he said.

"Yes, I will. You too," she answered, and quickly closed to door behind her.

For a long time she stood in her room, with her back against the door, still feeling his kiss on her lips.

True to his word, Hartley was waiting impatiently in the hall when she came down soon after nine-thirty the next morning. "I've finally met a punctual woman!" he explained. "I don't believe it!"

She grinned and leaned against him, gently nudging him with her elbow. They proceeded into the dining room where chafing dishes were set out for them. Everything smelled wonderful. She helped herself to scrambled eggs, sausages and bacon. After slathering her toast with lots of butter, she began to eat.

"I'm glad you have a good appetite," he said. "I loathe women who pick at their food."

"I'd probably pick, if I had a weight problem. But luckily I can eat whatever I like without getting fat. I wouldn't mind putting on a few pounds, if I could."

"You're fine as you are, Claire. Nicely curved in all the right places." He eyed her up and down. "I have a theory about women who have a good appetite and the correlation to sex. Do you want to hear it?" He smiled at her devilishly.

"Not particularly," she replied. "I'm sure I can speculate on your theory." She finished her coffee. "I'll get my coat and meet you at the front door."

"Wear a good pair of walking shoes."

She grinned and left him, rejoining him in the driveway a few moments later.

"I hope you're good for three or four miles," he said as they set off.

"I'll out walk you any day, Hartley Dale."

"Don't be so sure."

"I'm a small town gal. You're a city clicker!"

"You don't have much time for people who work in the big city, do you?" He asked.

"Are you passing the time of day right now, or leading with the chin?"

He stopped and looked at her squarely. "Leading with the chin. Tell me what you have against the city."

"It isn't the city as much as the system by which it works. It's far too easy for certain people to make a lot of money."

"Every country has its elite." Hartley said as he helped her over a wooden fence. "The former Soviet Union had its ruling class. China did too, although they would never admit it. At least they recognized that certain jobs and professions give people a different kind of status. Those with the highest status become aware of it and act accordingly. That's why there was a cultural revolution in China and since then, professors and scientists had to do their stints in the fields or factories to make them remember that they are no better than an ordinary laborer."

It was the most serious speech Claire had heard Hartley make, and she forgot her embarrassment with him and the strangeness of their association and was able to reply to him as if he were one of her own contemporaries. She only agreed with part of what he had said. As they continued to walk, she discussed this with him.

One hour became two and two merged into three before Hartley looked at his watch and stopped so abruptly that she bumped into him. He gripped her by the shoulder to steady her – and kept his arm around her. "It's one o'clock already! It will take us hours to get back."

"What time is lunch?" Claire asked.

"It's a help-yourself affair. Claire said that other people will be joining us for dinner tonight, but lunch is just casual."

"Then we don't have to go back for it. I'm sure we can find somewhere around here to eat."

Hartley looked around at the fields and trees around them. He looked at a loss. She giggled. "C'mon city slicker. There was a very small town that we passed about an hour ago. They must have some kind of a mom-and-pop restaurant. All towns do. You just have to know where to look."

The turned around and quickened their pace. In about forty-five minutes they came to a tiny town called Delisle. The main street held a gas station and a small grocery store which also doubled as a drug store. There was a postal box in front of the store. To the left hand side of the store was a restaurant – actually it was a glorified coffee shop. Inside were six tables set with wooden chairs. The menu was a handwritten card on every table. The card said "Lunch" at the top and there were four items written below. There were only two other people in the place.

"Now, this is quaint," Hartley remarked.

They ordered grilled cheese sandwiches with French fries and two large colas with lots of ice.

"Mmmm," said Claire as she drank half her cola at one time. "I was dreaming of a cold drink. And see? My dream came true!" She giggled and wiped her mouth with a paper napkin.

"Do you always make your dreams come true?" Hartley asked softly.

She paused and looked at him, touched by how earnestly he asked the question. "Well, I haven't had much time for dreaming. I've always been far too busy."

"You'll have plenty of time from now on, Claire. I hope that, during your time with me, your reality will be so pleasant that you won't want to waste time with dreams."

"Thank you. I hope so too," she murmured, relieved as the waitress arrived with their lunch.

Chapter 6:

Claire looked upon that grilled cheese sandwich lunch as the time when her attitude towards Hartley went through a subtle change. From the moment she had accepted his businesslike proposal of marriage, she had been aware of a vague regret that they had not met under normal circumstances, and had frequently wondered how their relationship might have developed had this been the case. But eating those golden-brown grilled cheese sandwiches together, she felt as though she was meeting him for the first time and – equally importantly – that he was seeing her for the first time too. In his black denim jeans, he looked like a small town guy much more than the Chief Executive Director of a vast investment company. He looked younger too, and this made her realize that he generally behaved far older than his age. No doubt it came from working with men who were usually twenty years his senior. Being long in the tooth seemed to be a necessary quality before one could achieve acceptance from the 'Old Boys Club'. She had always been aware of his quick wit but had not known it could be gentle and warm until he displayed it so well for their waitress, who was also the chef and dishwasher. In front of both her and her husband, who ran the general store and the gas station, he touched Claire's hand and smiled and was so charming that even she believed that they were a genuinely loving couple.

"When are you two planning on getting married?" the waitress asked them.

"Next Friday," Hartley shot Claire a quick glance. "I don't believe in long engagements."

"Will you be living around here?"

Hartley shook his head and popped another crisp French fry into his mouth. "We're just staying with friends this weekend. We're going to live downtown in Toronto."

"That isn't good for bringing up a family," the husband offered.

The waitress gave Claire an appraising look as though sizing up the chances that this petite, slim young woman had of being the mother of the children of this big strapping man. She must have come to a favorable conclusion because she nodded her head vigorously. "You really should get a place outside of the city. There are still reasonably prices homes if you're willing to drive an hour or so outside of Toronto. It's much better for raising children."

"I already have a home," Claire broke in, hoping to change the subject to the less embarrassing one of houses and mortgages. "It's just outside of Waterdown."

"Then I expect you'll be making your home there once your marriage has settled down. It generally takes a year before it does."

"You talk as if marriage were a fine wine," Hartley offered.

"It is." The husband moved closer to join the conversation, intercepting an amused look from his wife as he did. "Marriage is exactly like a wine. If it's a good one, it will improve with age. It it's a bad one, it will go sour."

"Yours will be a good one," added the waitress quickly.

Hartley gave her a grin that melted her heart, and took Claire's hand in both of his own. "How do you know that?"

"Not because I would dare to judge you," the woman stared directly at Hartley. "You're a type that I don't really understand and that's the honest truth." She then turned her eyes to Claire. "But your fiancée is as clear as water and has the ability to always get to level ground. You couldn't fool her and you are one lucky man that she has agreed to share her life with you."

Hartley's chuckle was deep and natural. Claire was intensely conscious of his nearness and of his hand still holding hers. She tried to release her fingers, but he did not loosen his grasp and, glancing into his face, she saw that his eyes were serious and had a far-away look.

Later, as they made their way back towards the Robertsons' house, he returned to the woman's comments.

"She is right about you, Claire. I'd never have thought to describe you as water, but that's exactly what you are."

"A shallow, babbling brook," she laughed.

"A still, cool river." Aware that she was breathing fast trying to keep up with his long strides, he slowed his pace and tucked her arm through his. She told herself that it was a gesture made to help her over the tall grasses in the field but she was touched by the solid feel of him. He gave her the impression of being more concerned with her own welfare than with others.

"Tell me about your house. You seem to be very proud of it," he asked her.

"I've lived there all my life so it's hard to describe. It is just home. I live in a very tight community and I love it. I look after elderly people and am involved in social work, helping out on distress centre phone lines in the township next to mine."

"Miss Do-gooder."

"I like it. It's very fulfilling work. Just because a person is old doesn't mean that you just stick them in a clinical nursing home or a geriatric ward and forget about them."

"What else can one do?"

"Lots of things!" she answered, incredulously. "I've been organizing fund-raisers and garnered enough money over the past three years to turn a very large, older home in Waterdown into a hostel for the elderly. People can have their own rooms yet know that there's always someone on hand to look after them if they need help or become ill."

"And that someone is you?" he questioned.

"Yes, me and another social worker."

"It sounds like a full-time job. How have you found the time to work for Miranda?"

"In my spare time. Plus, she pays me very generously."

"I suppose you're going to tell me that you use the money from her to spread a little happiness amongst the old folks?"

She saw the mocking tilt of his mouth and was furiously angry. Her eyes grew dark and her teeth bit hard on her lower lip to hold back the furious torrent of words that she wanted to unleash.

"You do?" he asked in astonishment. "My God, I was only teasing. You actually do give away the money that you get from Miranda?"

Still she did not speak and he gave her a little nudge.

"What on earth do you live on?"

"We raised enough money for the home to put aside a small salary for both me and the other social worker. Sometimes I don't take my salary but I take enough to live on." She refused to look at him.

"You're a fool, Claire," he said. There was no sarcasm in his voice this time. "I thought people like you died with the dodo bird."

"Then you don't know much about social work. No one who does it ever works for the money. It's totally at variance with your big bucks philosophy though."

He nudged her again. "I was wondering when you'd get back to putting me down. It's been two hours since the last attack."

Surprised at his remark, she stood still and turned to him. "I've never attacked you!"

"Not with words, perhaps. But, I wish you could sometimes see the look of disdain in your eyes. You make it very clear to me that you're contemptuous of what I do, and that you consider my job a waste of time."

"I am marrying you so that you can keep your job!" she reminded him.

"You are marrying me so you can get the money."

Quickly she averted her head but was aware of him watching her as if he were trying to fathom what was going on in her mind.

"Why are you so damn eager to help your cousin?" he asked her again. "You don't strike me as the sort of woman who would wallow in unrequited love."

"I've already told you that I don't love Charles in that way! I find that thought distasteful. We grew up together, almost like brother and sister and …"

"If you only felt cousinly affection you wouldn't be willing to sacrifice two years of your life in order to give him money for his business."

"Why not? You would never understand this situation, so stop asking me to explain it to you!"

"We're talking about two years of your life!"

"Two years is not that long."

"It can be a lifetime if you suddenly fall in love and want to marry someone else." He looked at her seriously.

"I'll take that chance." She dug her hands into the pockets of her trousers and wished that she could tell Hartley the truth. Yet, to an outsider, Charles' action would be construed as stealing so loyalty kept her silent.

"Well, I just hope you don't regret your decision," Hartley said softly.

"Why should I?" Determined to lighten the mood, she tilted her head up at him. "What makes you think it's such a sacrifice to marry you? You're not that bad. You're a very eligible bachelor, you know."

"Am I?"

She continued to stare at him. The pale sun still shone in the sky and, in its light, Hartley's hair glistened like it was streaked with silver. It was vibrant and slightly curly and Claire fought an urge to run her fingers through it. "I'm sure it wasn't necessary to pay someone to marry you. Lots of women would have done it for nothing."

"Would you have?"

"If I loved you."

"Then, it's a pity I didn't spend some time exercising my considerable charm on you," he replied. "I might have been able to save myself a lot of money."

There was a seductive edge to his teasing and she took a step away from him, aware that they were standing close together in a secluded area, close to the trees, away from the sight and sound of any other human being.

"My heart is too well protected to be bowled over by the likes of you," she said with as much composure as she could muster. "Anyway, we've already made our arrangements. Big business dudes like you don't renege on their business commitments."

His eyes narrowed and he looked incredibly sexy. "You're never at a loss for words, are you?"

"It's my only talent."

"I'm sure you have many others, Claire." He moved a step closer; his head low so that she could see the shadowed lids that partly hid his eyes. At close range, his mouth was more curved than she originally thought; its lower lip fuller and softer.

"Many talents," he repeated, and before she could guess what he was going to do, he pulled her to him with a gentle sweep of his arm and pressed his mouth upon hers. It was a soft, sensual kiss and she found herself responding to it, almost against her will. She was intensely aware of the warmth and strength of his body against hers. She could feel her breasts pressing against his chest and it thrilled her. As they kissed, he parted his lips slightly and sucked on her bottom lip very gently, lightly running his warm tongue against it.

He lifted his mouth away from hers, but still held her close. She suddenly felt very shy and refused to tilt her head up to look at him. She resolutely kept looking at the buttons on his jacket. The ground beneath her feet swayed and, with a gasp, she felt herself being lifted in the air until her face was level with his.

"Look at me Claire. Don't be shy. I won't do anything you don't want me to." He gently kissed her lips again and set her back down on her feet.

"Don't show off your male strength to me," she said, anxious to let him know that she felt confident again. "My father used to say that I may be small, but I'm indestructible."

He smiled. "I know exactly what your father meant."

He grabbed hold of her hand and kissed the palm lightly. They resumed walking. He seemed completely comfortable, almost as if he had forgotten that he kissed her only moments ago. She wished she could forget it as easily. But she could still feel the touch of his mouth on hers, the pressure of it still remained with her. She ran her tongue over her lips trying to duplicate the feeling of his kiss. More than ever, she found it strange that he was willing to lose his freedom in order to retain his important position at Farber. The Burnett Farber that she knew would never have made such a ridiculous stipulation, particularly since he had been fifty-seven years old when he married Miranda.

"Why didn't you call Burnett's bluff?" She hadn't even realized that she asked this question out loud until Hartley stopped and looked at her.

"What bluff?"

"His stipulation that you had to get married before you accepted the job?"

"He wasn't bluffing," Hartley said hesitantly. "And anyway, I didn't think it was worth my while to even take the chance."

"Is Farber Investments that important to you?"

He didn't answer at once, and she had the impression that he was reluctant to answer at all. Finally he did, though there was no expression in his voice. "What I've asked you to do is very important to me, Claire. Very important. I don't want to go into a long explanation about it right now. Just suffice it to say it is a pivotal decision in my life and career, okay?"

They left the Robinsons' place before dinner on Sunday evening. Even before accepting the weekend invitation, Claire had made it a condition that she was to be dropped off downtown by five o'clock. She did not tell Hartley the reason.

"Could you drop me downtown at the car rental place on King Street?"

"What for?" he asked.

"I'm driving out to Waterdown."

"You mean you're going home tonight?"

"Yes. I have to go back to work in the morning. I've only been able to spend so much time in town this week because I had some vacation days due."

"Why didn't you tell me that you wanted to return home tonight? I wouldn't have driven back all the way downtown. I would have taken the highway west and dropped you off."

"I didn't want to bother you. It takes just a little more than an hour to drive home and that place on King Street gives me a great deal for the car rental."

"You're being silly," he said, and started driving faster.

She watched the scenery fly past and then turned to him. "I'd like to talk to you about my work with the elderly. I meant to do so before but there hasn't been much time since the day I met you – I mean the day of our marriage is coming up fast. What I'm trying to ask is that … I guess that after we're married, you will want me to give up my job?"

"You guess right."

"Don't you think it's a terrible waste of my training?"

"Probably," he agreed. "But I need a full time wife."

"Only a temporary one," she reminded him.

"Yes, Claire. But it will be full-time for the temporary period."

"But I don't really want to do that," she said. "That would be asking me to give up a lot. And it doesn't seem fair. I mean, what are you giving up? Nothing! You only gain from this whole arrangement."

"I am giving up more than you know," he answered curtly. "Everyone has to make sacrifices."

"Well, I get a feeling that you aren't telling me the whole story regarding your sacrifice!"

They drove on in silence.

"I wish we could work something out Hartley," she began again.

"You mean you wish that you could talk me into agreeing with you!"

"Wow. Now that was an attack."

"I learn fast, Claire," he responded.

She felt defeated but still persisted. "I'm sure your home is extremely well run and that there won't be much for me to do. Can't I at least work part-time?"

"That wasn't part of your job description. But listen – if you can convince me that it won't affect your other duties, I will consider it."

"I'll only be able to convince you if you keep an open mind."

"My mind – like my life – is an open book."

"Yeah, but some of the pages are stuck together so people can't see them."

He laughed. "Ask me anything you like Claire. I'm not as secretive as you assume me to be."

"I think you are very secretive, actually." She searched his face, safe in the knowledge that his eyes were fixed on the road. "I mean, you're very attractive and obviously capable of wooing and finding a partner, yet when it came to it, you chose me. Now, what is that?"

"I've already told you that a marriage is compulsory if I am to rise up the corporate ladder."

"The corporate food chain is more accurate."

He laughed again. "You have a wonderful quick sense of humor. It's rare in a woman." And with that, the subject was closed – again.

Each time she had broached the topic, he had become withdrawn or evasive. She was now convinced more than ever before that there was an unhappy love affair in his life which he was trying to forget. This reason alone could account for his deciding to make this marriage a strictly impersonal one. She glanced out of the window and saw that they were speeding along the Queen Elizabeth Way.

"You aren't driving me all the way to Waterdown?" she asked in astonishment.

"That's exactly where I'm driving you. I feel responsible for you getting home safe and sound."

"I have driven a car before, Hartley!"

"Well, you are my fiancée and I am going to take care of you."

"Ah, well, it's official then, is it?" she asked.

"I think we can make plans, yes. I'm going to phone Burnett in the morning and tell him that, after a weekend in your charming company, I've decided that I can't live without you."

"Don't lay it on too thickly with Burnett. He isn't a fool. He's bound to guess you aren't the type to fall hopelessly in love with someone like me."

He did not answer, but she saw his hands tighten on the steering wheel and suddenly felt an overwhelming desire to meet this mystery woman who had made him fall hopelessly in love. But there was no point in asking him. He had already made it clear that he didn't wish to confide in her. Somehow she could not imagine him fully confiding in anyone. Despite his charm and obvious charisma, he gave away very little of himself. Even this weekend, when he had learned so much about her own background, he had disclosed very little of his.

She folded her hands in her lap and made herself comfortable for the drive home.

"I'm glad you know when to give in without arguing," he said. "I was expecting you to open the door and jump out."

"I'm no fool," she said matter-of-factly. "I'm delighted you're driving me home. But it's silly to make a long and unnecessary trip out of your way." She smiled at him.

He chucked. "Claire, you look very pretty when you smile. It makes me realize how serious you usually are."

She didn't answer but the first part of his comment remained in her mind for a long time. Did he really think she was pretty when she smiled, or was he just being polite? She longed to ask him what he thought of her but knew that to do it would be to invite teasing. Instead, she turned to the subject of their wedding.

"When is it going to be? I know you said next Friday, but ---"

"Next Friday. Twelve o'clock, at the Windsor Arms Hotel. We will then have a small luncheon in one of their private rooms."

"Will Miranda be hosting the luncheon afterwards?"

"Miranda?" He frowned. "What makes you say that?"

"Because she said she would. Don't you remember?"

"Ah, no," he shook his head. "Can't you talk her out of it?"

"I doubt it. After all, she feels responsible for our marriage anyway. I think she's looking forward to arranging the party."

"Do you?" he asked in such an odd tone that she was not sure what he meant. But he didn't elaborate and instead turned to the subject of their honeymoon. "To go away for an extended honeymoon is a bit of a farce, yet if we don't take a few days off it will look odd."

"And we don't want to look odd," she added sarcastically.

"No," he said shortly, "but we needn't go through the pretense of a month away in Europe either. I thought a week in Paris might do the trick."

"That's perfect," she replied coolly, but her heart was soaring. She was actually looking forward to spending some time alone with him. Two weeks would have been better. It would have been an ideal chance of really getting to know him. Quietly, she stared out the window.

"What's wrong?" he asked.

"Nothing."

"You're lying. Tell me the truth."

Giving him full marks for perception, she decided to be honest. "I was just thinking how nice it would be if we got to know each other. After all, we'll be seeing a lot of each other for the next couple of years and it would make things easier if we ...well, if we didn't feel like strangers."

"I don't feel that you're a stranger, Claire. In fact, I feel as if I've known you for a long time." He shot her a quick glance before turning his attention to the road again. "Is it part of your training to make people relax with you?"

"It's what a good social worker aims to do," she answered, "though I wasn't consciously doing it with you."

"What about subconsciously?" he teased, and slowed the car down, as if wishing to concentrate more on what he was saying. "This weekend you've kept bringing up the subject of me giving up my freedom for the sake of a job, yet you're giving up yours too."

"I have no regrets, Hartley. I've already told you that."

He sighed and the car gathered speed. In less than half an hour, they reached the city of Burlington. Twenty minutes more and they were driving slowly through the main street of Waterdown and Claire directed him to the small white Cape Cod style house where she had been born and had lived for most of her life.

"Will you stay and have something to eat before you go back?" she asked nervously as she led the way up the flagstone path to the front door. He nodded, and she went in ahead to switch on the lights. He loomed large in the front hallway and suddenly she saw her home through his eyes. Though she appreciated the few pieces of lovingly-cared-for antiques, she wished that the furnishings were not quite so shabby nor the carpets on the polished floors quite so worn. But it was a home which had been lived in, and loved in, and she gained comfort from this. Walking through the living room, she continued switching on lamps. In the warm glow, the room looked friendly and inviting and Hartley took off his chocolate brown suede jacket and dumped it on an armchair.

"Help yourself to a drink, if you like." She pointed to the sideboard. "I'll go into the kitchen and see what I can round up. I'm afraid it won't be much."

She was rummaging in the refrigerator when she heard his step and looked up to see him watching her.

"I wondered if you needed any help," he said and crossed the room to peer over her shoulder into the refrigerator. She felt uncomfortable and surprisingly excited by his nearness. He towered over her and so he easily was able to see into the depths of the fridge. She reached into the back and pulled out a huge golden crusted meat pie, a baked ziti casserole and a bowl of fresh, ripe tomatoes. "I thought you said you didn't have much food," he said.

"Mrs. Banister must have brought it in," Claire said as she also took out an open-faced apple tart, fragrant with cinnamon and cloves. "Yup, she sure did. This apple tart is her specialty."

She looked over at Hartley and he gave her such a quizzical expression that she felt compelled to explain that, whenever she went away for a few days, she left her house key with one of her elderly friends. Quite often, a few of them would drop by and leave her special tidbits they had prepared. It was their way of showing Claire gratitude and friendship.

"No wonder you don't want to give up your job here," Hartley commented later as they sat down at the table and devoured the savory, delicious meat pie, along with a portion of the warmed pasta and a tomato-and-onion salad. "This is as good a meal as I've ever tasted."

"I'll make it for you when we're married." She blushed the moment the words came out but knew it was hopeless to pretend that she had not said them. Besides, Hartley looked rather pleased at the prospect.

"I can't remember the last time I had a home-cooked meal."
"Don't you have a housekeeper?"
"Yes. But I eat out almost all the time."

"You've just had a weekend of home-cooked meals," she said.

"I meant in my *own* home," he chuckled.

Once again, his answer reminded her that she knew little about his background beyond the fact that he had lived an academic life before a corporate one. It seemed like a good opportunity to quiz him and she did so. For an instant she thought he wasn't going to respond to her questions, but the good food had put him in a mellow frame of mind and, after an initial hesitation, he started to talk about himself. His background was more unusual than she had imagined. His father's family had been an intellectual one while his mother's had been a prosperous one. It was in western Canada that he spent his formative years, dividing his time between a highly expensive private school and his grandfather's textile factory in Winnipeg, where he loved to work during holidays and where he had obtained first-class knowledge of the industry. His mother died when he was almost fifteen. It was at this time that his father decided to resume an academic life.

"Dad had worked for my grandfather's business from the time I was born," Hartley explained, "but when my mother died, he returned to Vancouver and remained there until his death just over a year ago."

"So you went to school there, and worked there at the University for many years?"

"Yes. Dad was disappointed when I decided to come to Toronto or 'the east' as he used to say, with disdain. I think he guessed that it was inevitable."

"At least he was alive to see what a success you became."

"Success?" Hartley echoed, and all at once looked bitter. It was as if the word evoked unpleasant memories. "If one equates success with money and business achievement, then I *have* been successful. But there are other ways of measuring success."

"I know," she said softly. "I wasn't sure that you knew."

He drew in his breath. "That was below the belt again Claire."

"I didn't mean it that way. But we were talking truthfully and I guess I didn't monitor my thoughts. They just dropped out of my brain and onto my tongue like a gum-ball machine."

He laughed out loud. "Oh Claire, you are good for the soul. Don't ever monitor your thoughts with me." Unexpectedly, he leaned across the table and softly rubbed the back of his hand against her cheek. "You don't know how much I welcome your honesty. It's a rare commodity in the business world and even rarer among women."

Her heart racing at his warm touch, she jumped up and busied herself at the stove making a pot of coffee. They sat in the living room chatting lightly. After they had finished their coffee, Hartley stood up to leave.

"When are you coming back into the city, Claire?"

"Well, it will have to be Thursday, since Friday is the wedding. It won't be easy for me to leave my job you know. It's awfully short notice."

"Your partners won't object, will they?"

She shrugged. "I have over four weeks' vacation due me and I'll take it in lieu of giving notice, I suppose. If I didn't have such a pivotal position in the collective, my name would be mud. You know that."

"I'm sorry," he said and touched her cheek again. He moved his hand down to her chin to lift it up so he could look into her grey eyes. "Incidentally, I liked your choice of clothes for the weekend. I particularly liked that red dress you wore on Friday night. It was quite becoming."

She smiled and looked up at him. As he bent down to kiss her on the lips, she turned her cheek to him at the last minute.

"Are we playing the shy girl tonight, Claire?"

"Having to keep you guessing Hartley," she teased.

"Thank you very much for the delicious dinner."

"My pleasure."

She saw him to his car and he briefly hugged her with one arm around her tiny shoulders. Watching him drive away until the tail lights of his car disappeared in the dark night, Claire reflected on the weekend. It gave her a better understanding of what made Hartley Dale tick and, though she knew there were many facets she did not know, she no longer felt as if she would be marrying a stranger on Friday at noon.

Chapter 7:

It was a bleak November day when Claire became Hartley Dale's wife and, signing her own name for the last time, she left the Windsor Arms Hotel as Claire Dale. Miranda and Burnett were their only witnesses but when they left the chapel and went to the private dining room, it was full of people, all of whom Hartley seemed to know very well. There was much joyful backslapping and teasing and Claire wished she had not let her fear of Hartley's sarcasm prevent her from inviting Charles. Sooner or later the two men would meet but it was not going to be on this auspicious occasion.

After an exquisite luncheon, many of their wedding guests were invited to go back to the Farber's house to continue the merriment. Momentarily alone beside the bar, watching everyone laughing and drinking around her, she wished she had allowed at least one member of her family to be with her on this momentous day. Even a marriage entered into for business reasons had something joyous about it. She sipped her champagne and saw a slim young man coming towards her. She had been introduced to him once, but could not remember his name.

"I'm James Farber," he said. "Burnett's nephew."

"Oh yes. Miranda has spoken to me about you,"

"I'll bet!" There was an inflection in his voice that inferred a deeper meaning behind his words, but he did not elaborate and she decided not to question him.

"Where are you two lovebirds going for your honeymoon?" he asked. "Or is it a secret?"

"No, it's not secret. We're going to Paris."

"City of lovers."

There was a sneer in his voice and this time it aroused her irritation. For the first time, she looked at him closely. It was easy to see his resemblance to his uncle. He had the same amber-colored eyes and tawny-and-red hair, though Burnett's was now mostly grey.

He was paler in complexion and very slender. It provided his face with angles and gave sharpness to his nose and chin. But it was not an unattractive face. It held character and a fearless way of looking at her that spoke of truthfulness.

"Have you known Hartley long?" He was speaking to her softly.

"No. Not really. We met here, as a matter of fact. Miranda introduced us."

"How clever of her!"

"Clever? I'm not sure I understand."

"For knowing what a lovely wife you would make for Hartley."

"Or for knowing what a suitable husband he would make for me," she responded.

"Let's hope you'll be able to say the same this time, next year."

"I'm sure I will – if I still know you by then."

"I work for Farber Investments, Mrs. Dale. I'm sure you're bound to see me frequently."

"Not unless you learn how not to make snide remarks."

For a moment, he seemed disconcerted by her attitude. Then, he smiled. It made him look even younger and she had the feeling that pure nervous energy was making him seem sharper than he really was.

"Are you married?" she asked.

"Not yet. But you're running true to form by asking me."

"True to form? I don't follow you."

He smiled. "All new brides like to try and marry off everyone around them."

"Well, perhaps we want everyone to be as happy as we are," she countered.

"Are you happy?" he asked.

"Of course!" His look was so intent that she had the uncomfortable sensation that he was reading her mind. "I think I'm very lucky to be married to Hartley. He's the kind of man many of my friends dream about."

"Is he the man that *you* dreamed about?"

"If he weren't, then I wouldn't be his wife today, would I?"

"Well, I'm not so sure Mrs. Dale. There are many reasons for getting married, and love may not be one of them."

"I'm sure that may be true in some cases. But why would you bring up that fact on my wedding day? If you're attempting to be funny, I find your sense of humor to be in extremely poor taste! Spit it out! What are you insinuating?" Claire was growing angry and impatient with James Farber.

"Actually I wasn't being funny, Mrs. Dale." He moved in front of her, blocking her from the rest of the room. "Honestly, I can tell the way that Hartley feels, but I must admit that you are a puzzle to me. If I didn't know better, I'd say you were genuinely in love with him."

"There you are Jamie!" Burnett had come upon them without being noticed. "Roger wants to have a word with you."

With another questioning look in Claire's direction, Jamie moved away and Burnett took his place, content to just stand beside her without talking. Claire was glad of his silence for she would have found it impossible to make coherent conversation, so bewildered was she by Jamie Farber's last words to her.

Instinctively she had rejected them, but like water on chalk, they permeated her and, in doing so, crumbled her strength from within.

She was in love with him.

What a fool she had been not to recognize where her feelings were leading her. Damn! She, who had prized herself on her logical mind and matter-of-fact attitude, had not even known what was happening to her. How could she? She had no prior experience with being-in-love on which to base her judgment. Even in her silly daydreams, she never even considered herself beautiful or bright enough to become involved with a man like Hartley.

It was only through a quirk of fate that they had come together and her irrational heart had gone out to him without her being aware of it. She sighed heavily. No matter how much she had deluded herself about her own feelings in the past two weeks, she was not in denial about Hartley's sentiments.

Alright! She might have fallen in love with him but she knew that he still saw her as the same person with whom he had arranged this business relationship. This agreement to become his temporary wife would enable him to further his career and ambition and then, when the time was ripe, she would fade from his life as quickly as she had come into it. If only she had known where her emotions would take her, she would never have agreed to Miranda's stupid suggestion! She would have turned tail and run for her life. But it was too late to run now; it had been too late since the weekend she had spent with Hartley at the Robertsons.

"I've never seen Hartley so relaxed," Burnett interrupted her reverie and she forced herself back to the present. "I think you'll be very good for him, my dear. He needs a wife and a proper home - somewhere where he can relax and be himself."

"Isn't he always?" she asked.

"Hartley? No. He wears a mask that few people can remove. But then I'm sure you know that for yourself already."

"I don't know that much about him," she said candidly. "After all, I've only known him a couple of weeks."

"You knew him well enough to marry him," Burnett smiled. "And you aren't a little girl, Claire. You're a woman – you're a wife – at least you will be very soon."

Claire blushed at the old fashioned way in which Burnett was alluding to the wedding night. She needed to ask him something. "Burnett? Were you surprised when Hartley told you that he was going to marry me?"

Burnett rubbed his finger along his upper lip and the gesture reminded her of his nephew whom she could see watching her from several yards away. "Hartley has always given me the impression of being self-sufficient – too much so sometimes. For that reason alone, I can say that I was surprised."

"Can one be too self-sufficient? I would have thought it is an ideal asset in the business world."

"It is a rare person who has no chink in their armor, my dear Claire. I'm delighted that you are the young woman who has found Hartley's."

Claire's gaze searched for her husband. *Her husband.* It was the first time she had thought of him in that way, but it was true. Regardless of how false their marriage was, he was still her husband. Standing beside him in the small chapel this morning, listening to the words of the marriage ceremony, she had been infinitely moved by them. She wondered now if Hartley had given them any thought or if he had closed his mind to them, seeing them only as the small unreadable print in their contract.

She stood erect, with her hands clenched at her side. This love she felt for Hartley awakened all sorts of foolish notions, not least of which was the hope that he might one day fall in love with her. On his own admission, he thought she was beautiful when she smiled. She certainly had the ability to hold his attention and amuse him. As far as a relationship between a man and a woman went, it was as good as any to begin with; probably better than most.

"If Hartley makes you unhappy," Burnett said softly to her, "you can always come to me for help. Sometimes he can be very tense and withdrawn. You are so young and vulnerable and may not know how to handle him."

"Not so young and vulnerable that it's stopped me from earning my own money and putting together my own projects, Burnett," she replied.

"You must not pester Hartley about his money, Claire," Burnett warned. "I know you have a social conscience but don't let it stop you from enjoying your life with him."

"I can't see myself being idle. That's just not my style."

"I know. I'm sure you won't be. And I certainly hope there will be children to keep you very busy."

The words brought such a vivid picture to her mind that she could almost see curly-haired toddlers racing on a perfectly manicured green lawn. She shut her eyes quickly and opened them again to force the image away. Burnett was not to be dissuaded and forged on:

"I'm looking forward to being a godfather to the first one, my dear."

"Give me time," she said weakly. "I've only been married for an hour!"

He laughed. "Take some advice from an old man. Don't wait too long! That's the mistake I made." His eyes grew pensive and sad and she knew that he was no longer in the room but somewhere back in the past. "Miranda was so young when I married her and I knew she wanted to travel and enjoy life and not be saddled with children. I thought that if we waited a few years by the time she turned twenty-six or twenty-seven she would find the responsibility less irksome. But, by then, of course, it was too late for me. Realizing how ill I was, I didn't consider it reasonable to father children that I might not live long enough to bring up."

There were many things that Claire could have made to this comment but since nothing could change the situation, she kept them to herself. To tell Burnett that she thought he had made the wrong decision or that Miranda had been selfish in not changing his mind, would have served no purpose except to hurt him or give him more regrets. So she murmured something that sounded like an acknowledgement and made herself look sympathetic. Inside, she was angry. Miranda had never shown much regret at not being a mother, had never even mentioned her childlessness in fact. Claire could not see her in a maternal role. She glanced around the room and found her talking to Hartley.

They made a striking couple, both tall and tanned; Hartley with his dark glossy hair and Miranda with her radiant red-gold tresses. There he stood tall and broad-shouldered making him look so strong, and there stood Miranda beside him, all five foot, eight inches of her – elegant and graceful. From a distance, she looked younger than her thirty years. Even close up, she certainly didn't show her age, but then the Mirandas of the world rarely did. They were so involved in their own affairs that outside troubles did not affect them at all. Even the problems that they might encounter always seemed to magically be taken care of by other people.

"I'm glad you'll be living in the city now, Claire." Burnett spoke up beside her. "It means that you'll always be there if Miranda needs you."

"Haven't I always been, Burnett?"

"Yes, but you'll be closer to each other now that you are married; emotionally and mentally closer, I mean. It isn't always easy for Miranda, you know. Her gaiety is an act, sometimes. There are many times when I sense her despair, anger and bitterness."

"Bitterness?" Claire repeated.

"That she can only count our future in months and not years; that we're both afraid to look too far ahead."

"But you are so much better now, Burnett," Claire burst out. "You haven't had a heart attack for over a year."

"Not a noticeable one," he murmured, "but several minor ones, and each time they do a little more damage. So the doctors inform me."

Her eyes filled with tears and she put her hand on his arm. It was difficult to think of Burnett, so tall and straight, so warm and kind to her, as being so ill that he was afraid to look beyond tomorrow. "I will always be here if Miranda needs me," she promised, "but I'm sure you will be with us for a long time."

"Thank you," he patted her hand and said, "come and let me introduce you to some of the other guests. I've taken up too much of your time."

She kissed him gently on the cheek. They moved around the room together, meeting people and chatting. She hoped with all her heart that she was not giving her true feelings away. How horrified Hartley would be if he knew that she was in love with him. Yet surely it would not take him long to guess? She had never been very good at hiding her emotions, had never seen the need for pretence. If she liked someone, they knew it. If she didn't, they sure knew that too.

She couldn't let it happen with Hartley. She had entered into this business contract with him and he wouldn't want the details of it to change. Yet this was what she was planning to do. Instead of being his temporary wife, she wanted to be his real one. This knowledge made her smile.

How astonished everyone in the room would be if they could read her mind. How bizarre this whole situation had become. Here she was, a happy young bride, plotting ways and means of making her new husband fall in love with her.

She glanced at her wrist watch. If she and Hartley were to catch the four o'clock flight they had booked for Paris, they had to leave for the airport very soon. She looked around for him but he was nowhere in sight. Thinking that he had gone to get his coat and start making his goodbyes, she went upstairs to Miranda's bedroom to collect her things.

Quietly she slipped away and ran up the stairs. She ran along the carpeted corridor. The sound of laughter from downstairs could no longer be heard and all was quiet. There was a heavy silence in the hallways. She reached Miranda's room and, opening the door quickly, ran in.

There was a man and a woman clasped closely together in a warm embrace. They were kissing each other passionately and did not have time to draw back when she entered the room. Still locked in an intimate clinch, they both looked at her.

Hartley dropped his arms from around Miranda's body and stepped back, looking directly at Claire. His face fell at the site of her pale face and open eyes.

The silence continued and Claire went on staring, frozen, at Miranda and Hartley as if she had never seen them before. The only thing that went on in her head was "*I'm so stupid. I'm so stupid.*" Over and over again. Finally, after and indeterminable length of time, she quickly crossed over to the bed, picked up her coat and headed back towards the door to leave.

The coat. It had been a wedding gift from Hartley. "A surprise for you" he had said as they left the Windsor Arms. It was beautiful faux fur – a designer label which she didn't recognize – but she was still duly impressed. It fit her perfectly and the dark coat went well with her creamy skin and dark grey eyes.

It was a lovely surprise.

And now he had given her another one!

In silence she continued on towards the door, but before she could reach it, Miranda was standing in front of her, barring her from leaving the room.

"Claire, let me explain."

"It isn't necessary."

"It is. You just don't understand."

"Of course I understand!" Claire cried out. "I'm not quite as stupid as you took me to be Miranda! I know exactly what game you're playing now. I know why you wanted Hartley to marry me. How could you?" she choked out. "How could you?"

"Claire, please," Miranda came close but did not touch her. "You have to listen to us."

The word 'us' infuriated her. It brought Hartley into this whole exercise. This was more than Claire could bear and she backed away. "You don't need to explain!" she burst out. "It's all too obvious. Burnett was beginning to suspect this extra-marital affair you've been having with Hartley and so, bringing me in as the little wifey was a marvelous decoy." She swung around and directed her stare at Hartley. "I don't know who thought of this plan but it's worthy of some kind of award."

"We didn't do it because Burnett is suspicious," Miranda said quickly. "He has no idea that Hartley and I – that we love each other. He regards Hartley as his friend and the man who will be taking over his company some day. It was because Jamie found out and so we had to …." Her voice trailed off. "Claire – surely you can see that we had no choice!" Her voice rose.

"Of course I see it!" Claire snapped. "It would have brought your little golden world crashing down upon you if anyone had found out that you were a cheating, faithless wife. It wouldn't have done your Mr. Dale any good either; the man who bedded the Chairman's wife to get to the top!"

"That isn't true!" Miranda cried. "You have no right to talk to me…."

"Let me handle this, Miranda," Hartley had regained his equilibrium and the control was back in his face. He looked over at Claire. "I can appreciate how you must feel. Finding me here with Miranda wasn't the most diplomatic way of letting you know the truth. I'm sorry it had to happen like this, Claire. I was going to tell you myself, but I intended to pick my time."

"Oh, yes?" she said bitterly.

"Yes, I was. Not that there was any need for me to discuss my private affairs with you."

"Affair being the operative word," Claire shot back.

His voice became unexpectedly harsh. "Look – our marriage is a business commitment and something that we both went into with our eyes wide open. My being in love with another woman does not alter the situation or the reason why you agreed to marry me!"

"Of course it alters it! It alters everything," Claire said furiously. "I would never have agreed to marry you if I'd known you were in love with Miranda Farber!"

"Why not?"

"Because…I….," she clenched her hands and turned away, knowing she couldn't possibly explain what was in her mind and heart. "It's the deceit," she continued slowly. "I suppose that people do get married purely for business reasons but this seems wrong to me. You married so you could continue to commit adultery with your boss' wife!"

"Do you think that Miranda and I want to live this way?" asked Hartley.

"Not that I care what you two want, but why this secrecy?"

"Because of Burnett," Miranda spoke again. "If he knew the truth, the shock would kill him."

She did not go on and Claire nodded, understanding what Miranda was saying. How clear that all was now; the reason for the marriage and the reason why she had been chosen. Little Claire who was so desperate for the money. Little Claire, who was Miranda's devoted little friend - always at her beck and call, still foolishly seeing her as the popular beauty queen at school and not as the patronizing benefactress that she truly was! And what a generous benefactress – bestowing her lover upon Claire until such time as she was free to take him back.

"Learning that Miranda and I are in love does not affect our bargain," Hartley continued. "My marriage is still necessary."

"And you're still being paid for it," Miranda added. "Don't forget how desperately you need that money."

Miranda's words were a triumph of diplomacy, reminding Claire of her own reason for the marriage and that it had been as pressing as Hartley's. Yet her reason had not been a deceitful one.

Or, was it?

The thought came into her head that perhaps that was not true. After all, Charles had stolen the money from his company and she was abetting him in the crime, just as her marriage to Hartley was abetting him in his adulterous relationship with Miranda. She glanced at them both, knowing that not one of the three of them came out well in this situation.

"I'll wait for you downstairs, Hartley," she said softly. "We have to catch a flight for our honeymoon. Please do not make your goodbyes too drawn-out?"

Without looking back at them, she hurried out. Only as she reached the end of the hallway did she stop and lean against the wall to try and still the trembling. If she had only learned about Miranda and Hartley a day ago, or even a few hours ago, it might have prevented her from ever succumbing to an awareness of her own growing love for him. An emotion, once discovered, could not be forgotten and no more could she be the new bride in love with, and dreaming of, a happy future with her husband.

For now the future lay with a cold, detached man; a man capable of living a lie, of being Burnett's friend, and of giving her a most soulful kiss last weekend. It was this that horrified her more than anything. Though she tried to see it from Hartley's point of view, she found it impossible. How could he justify the situation? She appreciated that Burnett's ill health prevented Miranda from leaving him but it made her sick the way in which the two of them were trying to get the best of both worlds.

The sound of laughter drifted up to her from the living room. She moved away from the wall and walked down the stairs. She had reached the bottom when Jamie Farber came into the hall and, after one look at her face, he came forward and whisked her away into Burnett's study.

"Sit down," he said, and as she obeyed, he went to the sideboard and returned with a brandy snifter which held a generous dollop of cognac. "Drink this. It will make you feel better."

Again, she obeyed and took a large sip. She was grateful that the liquid was in the wide balloon bottom of the snifter. Her hand was shaking so much that any other beverage would have slopped over the sides.

"What's wrong Mrs. Dale?"

"Don't call me that! Call me Claire," she said, regaining her composure. "Please." She hesitated and then sighed heavily. "I've ...I've just realized the meaning of your earlier innuendoes."

"I see." Instead of looking triumphant, he looked uncomfortable. "You really didn't know before, did you Claire?

"No, I didn't."

His face became softer, more attractive. "I never believed Hartley's story about love at first sight. I suspected from the start that he was getting married in order to keep me quiet. I just assumed that he had put you in the picture."

"Well, he didn't," she said shortly.

"I'm very sorry. I had no idea that you were genuinely in love with him."

"I'm not! I am not in love with him," she said harshly. "I am just disgusted by the deceit."

Jamie rubbed at his lip just as his uncle had done. It reminded Claire of who was really being so badly deceived.

"You are as guilty as Miranda and Hartley," she cried. "You forced them to take this ridiculous step."

"Now, hold on," he protested. "I never encouraged Hartley to do anything. I said he must either give up Miranda or leave the company."

"You must have said he could remain with the company if he married someone else."

"I didn't mean it in those terms., Claire. I meant that if he left Miranda and fell in love with another woman, and got married then

I would leave them alone. I never dreamed that he would cook up a phony marriage plan."

Claire stood up, holding on to her coat to keep it from slipping from her shoulders. The faux fur was soft and silky against her neck and smelled faintly of her own perfume.

"I have to go. It's getting late."

"Of course. I'll..." He stopped as the door opened and Burnett came in.

"There you are," Burnett exclaimed to Claire. "Hartley has been looking everywhere for you. You must hurry if you don't want to miss your plane."

Moving like a robot, Claire made her goodbyes to the well-wishing guests and then followed Hartley to the car. She must have been acting like the blushing bride since no one seemed to notice anything amiss in her actions or appearance, and she was even able to suffer Miranda's embrace at the front door.

"I'll talk to you when you return," Miranda whispered to her. "Please Claire, try and understand."

Claire could not bring herself to reply and she entered the car in silence. Hartley did not break it until they were well on their way to the airport.

"We'll have to talk about this eventually, Claire." His voice was brusque and formal. "We are going to be alone together in Paris for a week and we can either have a reasonably enjoyable time or turn it into a hell week. It's your choice."

"Perhaps it would be better if we didn't go."

"Getting married so quickly was enough of a surprise to my friends without also doing away with the honeymoon. I intend to carry on with all our arrangements. Arrangements," he added, "for which you have already been paid."

She thought of the certified cheque for fifty thousand dollars which had already been sent to her and then immediately cashed. Forty thousand dollars had been issued to Charles right away. He had driven to her friend's apartment last night to pick up the funds from her.

Charles had hugged her and said, "You'll never know how grateful

I am to you for doing this. I'll never be such a fool again. If I want to buy shares in the future, I'll do it with my own money, or not at all. Please Claire, you cannot ever tell Hartley Dale about this. I work in Toronto too, and if this ever got out…"

"I won't tell anyone," she assured him, and had found his overwhelming relief faintly irritating. Deceit was a characteristic she loathed, but now she had married a man who was a master in its practice.

She swung around to look at him directly. "I am not being your judge. I would have thought more highly of you and Miranda if you had only told me the truth."

"I did tell you the truth. I needed to get married for business reasons, and that still applies."

"You are playing with words Hartley." He didn't respond to this and her anger rose. "Wouldn't it have been more honest to just end the relationship with Miranda?"

"Jamie would not have been satisfied with that. If I wanted to stay with Farber Investments I would have to get married to someone else. It was either that, or leave the company completely. I don't know whether you've followed the fortunes of Farber but since I joined them, their profits have doubled. If I could find a way of remaining with them, I felt that I had to do it."

Though Claire tried not to be swayed by what he said, she couldn't help it and her anger abated. It was replaced by the anguish of knowing that she loved a man who only had eyes for another woman. Bitterly, she recalled her hopes of trying to make Hartley fall in love with her once she was his wife. It was one thing to believe she could fight a past love and an unknown woman. It was quite another to find out that the woman was Miranda and that far from being over, Hartley's feelings for her were still very much alive.

"Well, Claire," he said. "Can you understand why I did it?"

"Of course I can. In many companies, promotion only comes by stepping into a dead man's shoes and it's exactly the same at Farber. I see that clearly now. Except that when you step into Burnett's shoes, you'll also be able to sleep in his bed."

"My God," Hartley said quietly, "you certainly do know how to hurt someone, don't you?"

"Can you think of another way of putting it?" she asked sweetly.

He turned on her so sharply that she drew back, afraid for an instant that he was going to slap her. Then he relaxed, his wide shoulders lowering. "I know you like to call a spade a spade but for heaven's sake, you don't have to call it a damn bulldozer!"

"What on earth is that supposed to mean?"

"Sometimes the bluntest words can't begin to approximate the truth. You have obviously never been in love in your entire little life. You don't know what it can do to you. If you had even a glimmer of an idea, you would be much more understanding." He sighed. "I suggest that, from now on, we don't talk about this anymore. I'm willing to make our marriage obligations work as smoothly as possible, providing you play your part."

"I'll do what you've paid me to do," she said, and would have given every penny she possessed to have been able to buy back her heart. It hurt to know that she had given it to a bald-faced liar like Hartley who didn't even know he had it. He was a stranger to her. His understanding of loyalty differed from hers. His ability to simulate emotions was so brilliant that she felt she could live with him forever and never see beneath his stone-faced mask. It was an uneasy prospect.

"Yes, Hartley," she reiterated, "I will fulfill my side of the bargain, but just know that I will be counting the days until it's over and we can say goodbye."

"So will I," he said coldly. "Let's leave it at that."

Chapter 8:

Claire didn't expect to enjoy her stay in Paris but, to her amazement, she loved every glorious moment of it

In the evening, they arrived at L'Hotel Bassano, one of the most elegant hotels in the city, and were shown to the beautiful suite of rooms reserved for them. Hartley spoke perfect French, which made her own attempts to do so sound hopelessly inexperienced and silly. Not that it stopped her from trying – she rattled away to the chambermaid who came to turn down her bed. It was only when she came into the sitting room that divided her bedroom from Hartley's that she realized he had overheard her, for he was openly grinning.

"I don't know who deserves the medal," he said, "you for having the nerve to speak French to the maid – or the chambermaid for being able to understand it."

"I have courage sir. I am not faint of heart!"

"No, you're not. That is an admirable trait, darling wife." Realizing what he had said, he looked embarrassed, a fact which Claire noted with satisfaction.

"Where are we going for dinner?" she asked.

"Café des Etoiles," he answered.

"Well, we are certainly playing the part of the honeymooning couple well," she retorted. "A suite at the Bassano and dinner at one of the finest restaurants in the city."

"We won't be playing the complete part," he said softly, and his narrow-eyed look made it impossible to deny the meaning of his words. He had also said it to make her uncomfortable.

"Well, the only way we can make our arrangement a success," Claire said, sounding strong, "is not to try to embarrass each other."

"Well, aren't you a confident young woman!"

"Yes, I do feel confident today!"

"Have you had many lovers before?" he asked matter-of-factly.

She paused, only for a second.

"Only one," she replied, and then stopped, seeing his smile. "It was my first and only relationship. The fact that I am confident doesn't have anything to do with my lack of sexual experience," she continued in her haughtiest manner.

Smiling, he bridged the distance between them and came to stand directly in front of her. As always, his tallness overwhelmed her and she backed away from him.

"Please, Hartley, I can't stand it when you tower over me like that. It gives you an unfair advantage somehow."

"This advantage cannot be called unfair, darling. You're such a little spitfire that a mere mortal needs all the advantage he can get."

She forced herself to smile up at him, wondering what he would say if he knew he had a bigger advantage over her than any man ever had before. Just to be near him and to smell his warm clean skin turned her limbs to water. It made nonsense of her assertive voice. *I am allowing this physical attraction to blind me to his real character*, she thought weakly. *If he were ugly or scrawny I wouldn't think about him at all.* Yet it was not merely his looks that attracted her but the sharpness of his mind and his gentle, teasing manner. *What about the deceit?* Did that not matter anymore? That thought sobered her up quickly.

"I'll change my clothes and be with you in about half an hour," she murmured, and then went into her bedroom.

When she came out again, she felt more in control of herself. Hartley too appeared to have decided on a new plan of action, for he was attentive but courteous and treated her as if she were a distant cousin to whom he was showing the sights of Paris for the first time.

That evening set the precedent for the days that followed, as they explored Montmartre, visited the Flea Market and drove to Versailles. They went several times to the Louvre and the smaller galleries that were tucked into odd pockets of the city. These small galleries housed magnificent collections as well. They lunched or dined every day in the finest restaurants that Paris could offer.

Hartley regarded France almost as his second home. During his twenties, he had spent many summer vacations there and even after he came to work at Farber, he had flown to Paris at least twice. He regarded France as 'true civilization.'

Now seeing Paris again through Claire's innocent eyes, he discovered its delights anew. Her quick mind delighted him and he could not remember a time when he had been so amused and kept on his toes as he was by this petite attractive woman who had a tongue sharper than her mind. How furious she got when he teased her good-naturedly about her height – or lack of it. One evening, he laughed and said that he was going to tuck her into his pocket and carry her around. She had turned on him like a scorpion, causing him to make a mental note to be more careful in future.

Hartley didn't know why she would wish to be tall. Claire Evans was just perfect as far as he was concerned. Occasionally, when he sat across from her in a restaurant, he would think about Miranda and would fantasize about the time, in the future, when she would be able to sit opposite him instead.

But, as quickly as the thought entered his mind, he would try to dismiss it. Claire had sharp eyes and very little escaped her notice. Indeed, he was surprised by his desire to monitor his thoughts in this way.

On the day before their departure, he happened to mention it to her.

"It's a good thing that you're only five foot, two. As it is, you make me quake when you fix me with one of your stares!"

"Pfft. You're not scared of anything," she commented.

"I'm scared of you, Claire. You have such high ideals that you make my conscience prickle!"

She instantly became serious and he watched her face as she thought about this for a moment. A variety of expressions darkened her face during this time and he, for the life of him, couldn't figure her out. For a girl who could be so transparent, she was remarkable adept at hiding her feelings. He debated whether she had really come to terms with the way he and Miranda had deceived her. Perhaps she was only pretending in order to smooth the path of their temporary marriage.

"Claire, today is our last day and night," he said abruptly. "I want you to choose whatever you want to do."

"I want to have my hair cut and styled. The best hairdressers in the world are in Paris."

"Your hair looks fine to me."

"That's because you don't really see me as I am."

"Of course I do. What a thing to say!"

"Then, close your eyes."

"What?"

"Close your eyes."

"What on earth for?"

"Close them," she said. He did and then she said softly. "Now describe me."

Hartley was annoyed at having to play this silly game, but went along to keep the peace. "You are five feet, two inches tall. Your skin is pale and creamy smooth. Your hair is dark and shiny and soft. You have grey eyes." He went to open his eyes, but felt her cool fingertips on his lids.

"No, not yet," she said firmly. "I want a better description than that! How dark is my hair? How pale is my skin? What type of grey are my eyes?"

Carefully he allowed his inner focus to dwell on her, bringing forth all of his insight and acumen. He could not enlarge on the fine description he had already given. Taking his mind away from the first time he had seen her, he fast-forwarded his memory to the time when he first felt they were beginning to understand and know each other. That was the weekend they had gone to Jackson's Point to spend with the Robertsons.

They had gone for that walk on the Saturday, and had a simple lunch at the small restaurant. They had spoken with the husband and wife together and Claire had been smiling a lot that afternoon. Her smile was so pretty. Her hair had gleamed like sealskin. Her cheeks were like roses coming into bloom. Keeping his lids shut, he spoke again.

"Your hair is like the tropical sky at night, gleaming black and interspersed with points of light. You have luminous skin like a Botticelli angel and your eyes are like smoke. I can see the fire underneath that smoke. You have a Cupid's bow mouth, with a short upper lip that is extremely sexy. Your figure is ..." He stopped speaking as he felt her fingers lift off his eyelids.

He opened his eyes and stared into hers – at least as much as he could see beneath the veil of her long eyelashes. Her eyes *were* like woodland smoke, he thought. Looking at her from top to bottom, he noticed her features and her coloring and knew that she was exactly as he had described.

"Do you want to know how I see you?" she asked.

"No, thanks. I'd like to keep some of my illusions intact."

"I didn't think you had any."

"A man without illusions is a man without a soul."

She made a face and stuck her tongue out at him teasingly. "I refuse to have a serious discussion anyway. We were supposed to be talking about my haircut."

"No talking is necessary," Hartley smiled. "You may have the whole day free to get your hair cut, go to the spa, and go shopping, whatever you please. But, you must meet me for lunch at the Tour d'Argent."

"I don't need the whole day, just a couple of hours."

"Well, let's say four hours." He looked at his watch. "Meet me for lunch at one-thirty."

"Another light lunch at one hundred dollars a head?" she raised one eyebrow.

"Now you're talking like a wife," he teased.

Hartley wandered along the Champs Elysees, wondering how to fill in his time before meeting Claire again. It was very strange. He could not concentrate on anything. It was as if his mind were in limbo and his faculties held in abeyance.

There was a strange feeling of pleasure and sensual aliveness in his body. Granted, that should be normal on one's honeymoon but this was not a genuine honeymoon. Damn! If only this were real and Miranda was with him. The thought of her was suddenly so unbearable that he stopped at the next café and sat at an outside table. He ordered a café au lait and whisked out his cellular phone.

Within a few minutes, Miranda's voice came over the mouthpiece, husky and soft in his ear and making him throb with desire for her.

"I've been thinking of you this whole time," she purred, "and hating Claire for being there with you when I can't be."

"How is Burnett?" he asked. Then, he was horrified at the question and what it implied.

"Very tired. He hasn't been to the office at all in the last two days."

"I'm flying back tomorrow. I could back earlier if you needed me. All you have to do is call."

"Don't be silly, darling. You're on your honeymoon, remember?"

"I wish I could forget it," he said violently - a remark which seemed to please her for she immediately perked up and sounded much happier.

Hartley, on the other hand, felt even more unsatisfied after he hung up. Hearing Miranda's voice in no way appeased the longing he felt. It added to the burden of guilt he carried with him. How little Claire knew about him if she honestly thought that this deceit rested well upon his big shoulders. What would she say if he told her of the many hours when he had paced through the night wondering what to do about this relationship?

He frowned. He knew damn well what he had to do but lacked the strength of conviction to carry it out. Once Jamie had made his threats, he should have left Farber and never entered into this charade with Claire. His frown grew deeper. Once they returned home, he must make a point of meeting her cousin. What sort of man would allow someone he cared for to enter into such a commitment in order to provide him with the necessary capital to set up a business? He was still feeling contempt for this unknown cousin when he arrived at the Tour d'Argent and went up in the small elevator to the restaurant. He asked to be shown to his table and sat there, staring out at the city below and waiting for Claire.

Time passed and he glanced impatiently at his watch. One-thirty and Claire was nowhere to be seen. Like all women he had known, Claire obviously lost all sense of time once she got into the hands of a hairdresser. A faint stir at the end of the room drew his attention. A young woman had come in and was speaking with the head waiter. She drew the eyes of all the men, for she radiated beauty and vitality. Short black hair curled around her head and was feathered lightly around her lovely face. There were several fronds of hair curling forward on her cheekbones and they accentuated their fine angles. More tendrils caressed the lobes of her ears. Her slender neck was bare and she had on a figure-cutting black Chanel suit. The dark suit gave a glow to the woman's coloring along with her smoky eyes and the lovely shade of raspberry lip gloss she was wearing. Her complexion was startlingly beautiful. She had skin the color of mother-of-pearl. The pert head turned fully towards him and he swallowed his astonishment. Hartley realized that he had been staring at his own wife!

Even after she sat down and ordered a glass of champagne, he could not take his eyes away from her face. It was incredible that a haircut could make so much difference to her appearance. But it was more than just a restyling of her hair. She was wearing an outfit he had never seen before and her make-up was totally different. Her eyelids were delicately shaded in violet and grey. They looked twice as large as he had remembered. Her eyelashes were long and thick and he briefly thought she had on false ones but as he leaned towards her, he realized that they were her own. She was also wearing that amazing raspberry lipstick which made her full mouth look soft and moist. Suddenly he was reminded of Miranda's mouth and the feel and taste of it. He fought to gain control of his thoughts.

"You look different," he said lightly.

"Do I meet with your approval?"

"You must know that you do. No woman who can glide across a restaurant with so much poise needs to be told how lovely she looks."

"I must say that I am pleased with myself," she confessed. "But I'm afraid it's going to cost you a fortune. Hope you don't mind." She giggled and sipped at her champagne.

He laughed. "I'm glad that you have no false modesty about spending my money."

"You can afford it, darling," she said calmly.

"Yes, quite easily."

"I propose a toast," she said, lifting her glass. "To the new me, and also to a new life and new attitude upon our return home."

Warily, he looked at her but her expression was blank.

"Our stay in Paris has been like a prologue, don't you think?" she asked. "Once we are settled in our home, then the proper play will begin."

"And it will continue until the curtain comes down upon the final act." He added.

"Of course. When Burnett is dead. Then it will be curtains for us, won't it?" She smiled sweetly. "Don't bother to deny it."

"I wasn't going to." He saw her flush and wished she could be more realistic about Burnett's ill health. In the beginning when he first realized his love for Miranda, he had also been sensitive to Burnett's situation. Stepping into a dead man's shoes – the words popped into his mind and he angrily pushed them back out. Damn Claire! Why did she have to bring such a thing up?

"Let's order lunch," he said, with a calmness that he did not feel. "And more champagne."

Claire half smiled but remained quiet. She felt the change come over him when she had mentioned Burnett's name. She could have held her tongue but decided to again call a spade a spade. Changing the subject, she started to tell him about the two hours she had just spent at the hairdresser, and the two hours in the exclusive shops on the same boulevard. Soon, Hartley was smiling at her descriptions.In short time, he was laughing openly as she mimicked the young man who had styled her hair. She put up a hand to touch it, still not used to the shortness.

"Do you like it?" she asked.

"Very much. And I like your suit too."

"I bought some other things as well," she confessed. "On our way back to the hotel, I still need to pick them up. I was only able to pay for this suit so I left the rest on deposit."

"Certainly, I have my credit cards with me. How much did you spend?"

When she mentioned the sum, which she considered astronomical, he didn't even blink an eye.

He nodded at her and his only comment was, "If you want to get anything else, there will be no problem."

"Things are very expensive here, Hartley."

"But much smarter. Go out, have fun, buy whatever takes your fancy."

"Will you come shopping with me?"

"I have a few calls to make." He hesitated. "I thought I would call Burnett. He isn't well."

Claire knew then, without being told, that he had already spoken to Miranda. She felt such a wave of dejection that it was all she could do to continue eating. She had still not overcome this feeling when they left the restaurant, though once she had said goodbye to Hartley and set off to do her shopping, her spirits were revived. If he ever realized how the thought of Miranda spurred her to uncharacteristic extravagance, she thought as she recklessly bought one outfit after another in an exclusive little shop on the Faubourg St. Honore, he would never mention her name again!

Despite herself, the idea of this made her smile and the vendeuse, assuming it to be satisfaction with all her purchases, offered her more and more of the dresses and accessories.

"Madame is so easy to fit," she chirped. "Not as tall as a model, perhaps, but so slender. Shortening a hem is very easily done."

Claire allowed herself to be talked into several more purchases and then gave the address of the hotel where they were to be delivered. It was almost five o'clock when she returned to her suite, exhausted, and soaked for a long time in a hot bath. She then rang for the maid to unpack the things she had bought and then repack them in the set of cream-colored Louis Vuitton luggage to which she had also treated herself.

"Please leave out the black chiffon," she said. "I want to wear it tonight."

Claire had never considered herself to be demanding or pampered but when she emerged from the bathroom, warm and perfumed, to enter her rose-shaded bedroom and see the black silk lingerie on the bed, the black dress floating on its hanger in the wardrobe and raw silk wrap lying on the back of the chair, she became aware of how easy it would be to succumb to luxury. She experienced a pang of guilt at the knowledge that the money spent on this outfit alone would keep one of her old pensioners for almost a year. The realization that she wouldn't have spent such a vast amount on clothing had she not been angry with Hartley for deceiving poor Burnett only added pepper to her actions.It was an empty vengeance.

Damn both Hartley and Miranda! They had played her for a fool and now she was going to take full advantage of the part they had created for her. She would not be playing it for long, so she might as well enjoy it while she could. But she must not allow herself to lose her social conscience. She didn't want to turn into a snob like Hartley Dale who could turn a blind eye to the less fortunate and not give it a second thought.

Did he ever think of others, or was he so wrapped up in himself and the world of high finance that he had no time to spare for the millions around the world whose daily existence was focused solely on survival? It was a question she would love to ask him, but she had to wait for her moment.

Pushing these thoughts aside, she stepped into the black chiffon. The skirt whispered softly against her, falling wide from a tightly nipped-in waist. The bodice was tight and the black silk lining barely reached the curve of her breasts, leaving the rest of her skin to be covered by the gossamer-fine chiffon. The sleeves were short, coming just off her shoulders in an angular cut. Careful not to muss the fragile material, she tried to zip the back, but she could only reach her waist, for the rest of the back was fastened by tiny buttons. She rang for a chambermaid, wishing she had had the foresight to tell the one who had been doing her room to come back to help her. While she waited for the young woman to arrive, she finished her make-up and hair.

She loved the way it bounced with every movement of her head and the way the curly wisps framed her face, making it look heart-shaped. This, in turn, made her eyes appear larger.

She stared at her mouth, wishing it was more voluptuous; a short upper lip made her look like a child. Claire was too used to it to realize how sexually provocative it was.

Hartley, walking into the bedroom, was fully aware of how sexy and provocative his wife's beautiful lips were. He was also aware of how glamorous she looked. She would, one day, make some man a wonderful wife. Then, with a shock, he realized that she was his wife, and he could not help experiencing a twinge of sadness that such loveliness was wasted. Claire should have married someone who loved her; someone who would care when her eyes shone at them. Some man who would want to kiss that smiling, mischievous mouth. Not that he would object to kissing her, he thought idly and because that thought was unfair to Miranda, he pushed it away.

"I'm sorry to barge in, Claire," he apologized. "I thought you would be ready."

"I am. I had just phoned for someone to come up and help me with the buttons on the back of my dress."

"May I help you?"

She hesitated and then turned her back to him. "The buttons are very small," she said. He did not reply but she felt his warm fingers on her skin as he began to fasten them. She tried not to be conscious of how close he was, but he was so near that the slightest movement on her part caused her to feel his body.

"There," he said when he had finished. She detected a faint tremor in his voice.

She turned around. "How do I look?"

"Do you really need me to tell you?"

She smiled brightly as she turned to pick up her wrap. There she stood, her face framed by the dark colors of the dress and wrap, her skin gleaming like pearls. Her jet black hair was as lustrous as a raven's wing and her large grey eyes shone with excitement.

"You're a very beautiful woman, Claire," he said, softly. "I'm sure you already know that."

"A woman always likes to be told."

He took her arm and tucked it beneath his. "I'm going to be the envy of every man who sees me tonight."

"It's a good thing they don't know we're only play acting, then."

He turned to face her. "Don't say that!"

"Why not? It's the truth."

"It isn't. When I told you how lovely you look, I meant every word of it. I just regret that – that this honeymoon can't be real ...for you."

She grew warm and the flush on her cheek brightened. Had Hartley guessed that she was in love with him? She hoped not since she used every fiber in her body to convince him otherwise.

"You deserve to be married to a man who will love you and cherish you in every way; emotionally, spiritually and physically," he continued. "Not someone like me who can only offer you ..."

"A pay cheque?" she interrupted. It hurt her heart to say this. "Hartley, I appreciate this sentiment, I really do. Just because I seem sweet and innocent to you doesn't mean that I am a child. We both went into this marriage contract for our own reasons. Those reasons still apply."

He looked at her with an emotion on his face that she couldn't detect. "They shouldn't have applied for you."

"Well, I don't want to discuss it."

"Very well Claire. I won't mention it again."

For the rest of the evening, Hartley made every effort to be charming and entertaining. Claire could almost believe that she really was a bride on her honeymoon. If only this make-believe were true. She briefly allowed her fantasies free rein and wondered what kind of lover he would make; experienced, of course, and masterful, but she knew that he would be kind, tender and sensuous too. He had only kissed her once and there had been nothing inexperienced about him. His touch was callow and she knew he would be skillful at rousing a response from her. But she knew instinctively that he would also be very patient and take the time that she needed.

"You're staring at me with a very curious look in your eyes, Mrs. Dale," he teased, interrupting her thoughts. He raised one eyebrow at her and watched her blush pink before his eyes. "My! What kind of thoughts were they? Dare I ask?"

"I was imagining what kind of lover you would be. I was fantasizing how it would be to make love with you."

As she said this, he was taking a sip of red wine which came spluttering back into his glass. He looked at her and set the glass down on the table. "My God, Claire! Will you ever stop surprising me? You're shameless, do you know that?"

"Don't be silly. You're not that easily shocked." She waved him off, trying to seem calm so she wouldn't throw herself into his arms. "However, I would be shocked if you hadn't thought the same thing about me. You may be in love with Miranda but you're not blind to other women."

"I'm not blind to *you*," he added.

"Well, of course not, with thousands of dollars of fine plumage on me!"

"Don't underestimate yourself Claire. I noticed you a long time before you spent my money on those fine clothes. You are not a woman that a man can ignore."

"I'm no beauty."

"Aren't you?" He looked at her longingly and the blueness of his eyes seemed electric. "You are not only beautiful Claire, but I imagine you would be a willing and explosive lover."

"Well, not explosive in a destructive way, I hope," she laughed. He took her hand in his and held it. She could feel herself trembling.

"I'm not sure about that. You may be destructive to men's hearts." He signaled to the waiter that they were ready to order dessert and coffee and she took the opportunity to pull her hand away.

He looked down at his napkin. "Claire, if you have no objections, I would like to catch an earlier plane tomorrow. I need to get back to see Burnett."

"For business or personal reasons?"

"What do you mean by that?"

"Don't you know?" she asked scornfully, hurt pride making her speak when she knew she should be silent. "Do you want to see how Burnett's health is because you care about his welfare or because you want to know how soon your Miranda will be free?"

"Damn you, Claire!" he exploded. "Don't you know when to shut up?" He couldn't believe that he had lost his usual calm with this woman. She pushed him right over the edge!

She stared down at the tablecloth and was mortified to feel tears spilling down her cheeks.

"Don't cry!" he said roughly. "That would be too much."

"I'm so sorry. You have every right to be angry with me." She wiped the tears away with the back of her hand and looked at him, forcing herself to smile. Tears glimmered in the corners of her eyes and she looked so heartbreakingly young and tender.

"I don't want to hurt you," he whispered. "We should never have done this. This whole marriage idea was a mistake. You're not ready to take on an assignment like this."

"I think I've done very well so far, Hartley." She was determined not to let him take pity on her. "Just bear with me for a little longer. I promise I won't lose my temper again."

"Don't make a promise you can't keep!"

They both laughed at this and it broke the tension. There was still something she had to say. Getting up her courage, she forced herself to ask, "If anything should happen to Burnett – I mean sooner rather than later, I would be prepared to leave right away. I don't want you to worry about gaining back your freedom. I'll leave whenever you say."

"Thank you. I appreciate that."

"Hartley Dale? What the hell are you doing here?" A booming voice broke in on them and Claire looked up to see a handsome, white-haired man in his middle fifties.

He was standing there, accompanied by an elegantly dressed woman along with another couple. They were all smiling and had obviously had a lot to drink with their dinner. They appeared to know Hartley very well and suggested that he join them at a night club for some dancing and fun. Hartley looked over at Claire. She loved the idea of going out somewhere else because she didn't relish the idea of going back to the hotel and lying awake all night with her thoughts. She nodded enthusiastically.

Claire had never been to a night club before. A downtown dance club was the nearest that she had come to it, and that was a far cry from the dreamy, sophisticated interior where the music was soft and jazzy and champagne or cognac seemed to be the only beverages available.

The dance floor was huge with plenty of room to maneuver. She hoped that Hartley would ask her to dance. It was something she had looked forward to for so long. When he finally asked her, it was almost anticlimactic and she sighed with pleasure as they glided onto the dance floor. Hartley's arms were around her and she didn't have any feeling of anxiety or tension. As a matter of fact, it felt very comfortable, almost like coming home.

He heard her sigh as he pulled her closer. "We don't have to stay long if you're tired. I thought you might like to come for a little while."

"Are you kidding? I love dancing. This is wonderful."

"Do you dance much?"

"No, not since I left university. There was a group of us that used to go to a dance club down near the lake. We would go early before they charged a cover fee and just have a couple of beers." She laughed lightly. "It was another world away from this."

"Claire? Why don't you live in Toronto permanently? You could find a high-paying job anywhere, with your degree and your qualifications."

"I've already told you why I won't leave my home. I feel it is a duty to stay and help my retired folks. That sounds so Suzy Do-Gooder, I know, but it's how I feel."

"I don't see you as a do-gooder, not anymore. You're very honest and you say what you feel." He held her even closer and smelled the fragrance of her hair. There was a tightness in his chest as well as in a lower location on his anatomy. He heard the song end and the new music had a quicker pace. It gave him an excuse to pull away.

"This is not my style. I like slow dancing." He started to lead her back to their table when a young man stepped in front and murmured something in French to Hartley.

"Well, he wants to cut in," he said to Claire. "Do I hit him or let him dance?"

"I'll dance with him," she said quickly and gave the young man such a wide smile that he forgot to thank Hartley for the loan of his dance partner.

For the next twenty minutes, Claire gave herself up to the pure joy of dancing. She had rarely had the opportunity of doing so in the past few years and had forgotten the thrill of allowing her body to find its rhythm. In this dim Paris night club, it made the past seem like eons ago. She was living in this exciting, pulsating moment and when she finally returned to the table, she was breathless and flushed.

"I hope you don't mind?" she said as she fanned her face sitting beside Hartley.

"Not at all. I enjoyed watching you," Hartley said, adding in his mind. *It also gave me a chance to gain control over my body.* "Well, you seem to have an admirer. Your dance partner is looking in your direction again."

"Well, he's wasting his time," she said. "I'm ready to go back to the hotel. I'm feeling tired now."

Hartley stood up and bid good night to his friends who seem to have settled in at their table for the evening. Knowing them, they were parked until the wee hours of the morning, he thought. Arriving back at their hotel, they waited for the elevator. Claire seemed to be totally exhausted and her feet were hurting her. She took off her shoes in and held them in her hand. Her chiffon skirts swayed around her as they slowly padded along the carpeted hallway towards their suite.

"Poor tired little lamb," Hartley murmured and swung her up in his arms and carried her the rest of the way into their living room, kicking the hotel door behind him. He didn't stop there, but carried her all the way to her bedroom and dropped her gently onto the bed.

She lay back on the pillows.

"Thank you so much Hartley. It was a wonderful evening", she said, and she held up her hand to him.

"I would like to thank you," he said as he caught her fingers and bent forward. Unaware that he was going to come towards her, she raised herself up to say good night and found her face almost touching his. In a smooth motion, he pulled her all the way toward him and kissed her lightly on the mouth. Then, he released her hand and, putting his arms around her, pulled her against his body. His hands were warm on her back and she felt him running his fingers up and down her spine.

Claire knew that she should resist him, but it was impossible. She wanted him so badly. Her hands came up behind his head and pulled him against her neck, feeling his soft, curly hair between her fingers. She moaned and he kissed her neck, giving a sound of satisfaction. Shaking with emotion, she pulled her head back to offer her mouth to him again. He took it and, savoring the taste of her lips, kissed her deeply. Instinctively, she offered him her tongue and he sucked on it lightly.

Pushing her down on the bed, she felt the weight of his body on top of her. He pulled himself up on one elbow and cupped her breast gently in his hand, teasing the nipple with his thumb. She was aware of how quickly she was breathing and the way her heart was thumping in her chest. Never had she experienced such a feeling of sexual excitement before.

Looking into his face, she could see the dark excitement in his eyes. He bent down again to kiss her neck and throat, his breath coming warm and heavy upon her skin, through the delicate chiffon. His mouth traveled down to the curve of her breast. The dress was in the way, and he turned her on her side to quickly undo the buttons and zipper behind her.

Pulling the dress down to her waist, he resumed his attentions on the creamy peaks of her breasts. Shivering with pleasure, Claire again made a mewling sound, unable to keep silent. His fingers danced along the skirt of the dress pulling it up to expose her legs. He traced his fingers along the inside of her thigh and could feel the gooseflesh developing there. Pulling the skirt up, his hand was on her black silk panties and he slipped one finger underneath the crotch of the panties to feel the warmth of her womanhood. As he teased the pink peak of her breast with his tongue, he smiled to discover the soft and swollen inner folds all slippery and moist.

Claire thought she would faint dead away from the pleasure of his touch. She spread her thighs wider and pressed her head back against the softness of the pillow.

"Oh, Miranda," she heard him whisper.

With a gasp, Claire wrenched free of his embrace. She felt as though someone had thrown a bucket of ice water on her body. All she knew was the pure hot anger of betrayal she felt at this moment. She was so stupid! Wanting Hartley so badly had made her forget all about Miranda.

And Hartley! That little weasel had been roused in passion, yes, but subconsciously he was holding the woman he really loved in his arms, not her. His used of Miranda's name had proved this beyond all doubts she may have had.

She felt numb. "Please, go." Her voice was thick, but she forced herself to stay calm.

"Claire. Forgive me." He felt dreadful, and deflated.

"No, please. Don't apologize. It was my fault. I forgot how small men's brains truly are!"

Abruptly he strode across to the door and did not look back at her as he closed it behind him.

Chapter 9:

By the time she awoke the next morning, after a fitful sleep, he had packed and was gone. Thankfully, Hartley had arranged for the chambermaids to pack her things, and a driver to take her to the airport for she was barely capable of doing those things for herself.

When she arrived back in Toronto, a chauffeur driven limousine picked her up and drove her to her new home. It was one thing to be Hartley's wife on a trip to Paris, but it was quite another to share his residence where every object and every room brought him to mind constantly. The days passed slowly. Without her work to take her mind off things, time hung heavily in the air. She had frequently envied Miranda the life she led, but faced with it herself, she found it empty and boring. She hated it.

Miranda! The very name brought with it memories of being in Hartley's arms. Claire was honest enough to admit that this would forever affect her relationship with a woman she had considered her friend for years. Yet, had they really been friends? School girl relationships were usually fleeting and dissolved after the graduation party. Whatever it was that had existed between them, it existed no more. It was painful to admit that Miranda had used her, but it was true. If there had been a true bond of friendship between them, Miranda would never have allowed her to marry Hartley without telling her the truth behind hit. Now that her eyes were wide open, Claire saw things all too clearly.

This was the most painful lesson of becoming Mrs. Hartley Dale; the knowledge that she had given her friendship to someone who had not deserved it.

Within an hour after returning from France, Hartley had gone to visit Burnett. He had gone over to the Farber's house daily after that. Each time Claire had been invited and each time, she pleaded exhaustion and had remained in the penthouse, using the time to settle herself in the spare bedroom. She wanted to make this space her own for the time that she was living in Hartley's home.

She was sure that Hartley noticed the true reason she didn't want to go with him. Always sure to inquire about Burnett's health, she deliberately refrained from ever mentioning Miranda's name. Intentionally, Hartley saw fit to indeed mention her and Claire always ignored it.

The sad news was that Burnett had suffered another heart attack and so had been advised to take it easy for a month. It seemed that he was only buying time and knew it, for he had insisted that Hartley take over much of his responsibilities and learn all the affairs of the company.

"I didn't think there was much more that Burnett could teach you," she remarked one evening.

"We don't talk about day-to-day events," Hartley admitted. "Burnett enjoys talking about the past and I indulge him. That's why he asks me to come over every day. He's telling me the whole history of the company and how he built it up from scratch. As well, he's introducing me, via conference calling, to some new players in the New York office."

"And how is Jamie? Does he seem to resent you for being the Chief Executive Director, instead of him?"

"I'm sure he does. But he's far too young for the job. The thing is that some people think I am too at the age of thirty-four. But they seem to feel that I have sufficient authority and he doesn't. He's resentful because he knows everything about running the company and knowing how it works. But it takes more than that – you have to possess massive energy along with the ability to inspire others. James doesn't have it in him."

"I'm sure you are an inspiration to everyone who works for you."

Her sarcastic tone was not lost on him and he looked at her sharply. She returned it with a wide-eyed, innocent gaze. He let it go.

It was not until a week later that he told her that Miranda and Burnett had invited them to dinner. She longed to refuse the offer, but it was impossible. To do so might make Burnett suspicious and also break the bargain she had entered into with Hartley; to act the part of his wife and attend with him on social occasions such as this. She was smart enough to know that her reluctance to accept the invitation stemmed from her aversion to see Miranda but she didn't have to make Burnett suffer with the loss of her affection and friendship. So she went.

Miranda's greeting was as warm as ever, but her eyes could not hide the astonishment at the change in Claire's appearance. No comment was made until Burnett mentioned something. It brought an immediate frown, which was quickly disguised to a look of surprise, on her lovely and perfect face.

"Marriage certainly agrees with you, Claire," Burnett exclaimed. "You look absolutely enchanting."

"Thanks to an exquisite week in Paris, along with a new hairdresser and new clothes," Claire smiled.

"Well, to say you've turned into a beautiful young woman implies that you weren't lovely before, but I …," Burnett stopped.

"On the contrary," Hartley said as he came in to stand beside Claire and put his arm around her shoulder, playing the part of the loving bridegroom. "She was pretty before, but is now gorgeous!"

"Well said," Burnett agreed. "Hartley, would you play host and make cocktails for everyone before dinner?"

Hartley did so and looked so at home mixing drinks at the sideboard bar that Claire felt sickened. How clever he and Miranda had been pulling the wool over Burnett's eyes. Again, she wondered why he had allowed himself to become involved in such a despicable situation. The heart could not be guided, that she knew, but it would have been better to leave Farber than to live with this deceit every day. She didn't believe he had refused to do so because he was afraid of being unable to find another position of equal importance. This led her to the conclusion that Miranda had forced him to stay.

She studied Miranda, bitterly acknowledging that her beauty alone was probably enough to make any man lose his senses. Reed-slender and elegant, with perfect flawless skin, she was a picture of sensual delight. No wonder Hartley was her devoted slave; loving her so much that he was prepared to live a lie. This had not only indicated his strength of mind, but also the depth of the passion he felt for her. It was deep enough to destroy his sense of right and wrong.

The door opened and Claire's fingers tightened on her wine glass as she recognized James Farber. Accepting a drink from Hartley, he sat down beside her. Tensely, she waited for him to speak, anticipating some snide comment of her honeymoon. She was not wrong, for it came immediately.

"I'm glad to see you didn't totally waste your time in Paris sulking in the hotel room," he whispered to her. "You took advantage of the shops!"

Claire pursed her lips and took a small, deliberate sip of her drink. She was wearing one of the Paris dresses; it was a beautiful cobalt blue dress with long sleeves and a tight skirt, making her legs look long and lovely. "If you want to start a verbal debate with me, Mr. Farber, I'd better warn you that I'm very good at it. I was head of my Debating Society in university."

"Oh, very impressive, Mrs. Dale. Is that supposed to frighten me?"

"It should – if you know what's good for you."

He flushed in irritation and it made him look younger and less unsure. Though she guessed him to be in his mid-twenties, she felt years older than him. The cool confidence which exuded from her made Jamie lose his edge.

"You got what you wanted," she whispered to him. "Hartley has a wife and he isn't seeing Miranda any more."

"You are so naïve. Do you believe that he'll remain faithful to you and not see Miranda anymore? Or will he use you as a cover while he and Miranda carry on as before? I've a good mind to let Uncle know the truth!"

"You would never do that."

He looked at her. "What makes you so damn sure?"

"Because you wouldn't want to live the rest of your life knowing that you may have pushed Burnett over the edge and caused his fatal heart attack. You know how sick he is. He couldn't withstand the shock."

Jamie didn't reply but the way he avoided her eyes told her she had scored. The knowledge made her wonder if Hartley had tried to call Jamie's bluff. Still, if he had done so, she would not be here now, married to him and in love with him.

"You're quite right, Mrs. Dale." Jamie's voice was barely audible. "I would never do anything to hurt my uncle. You'd do well to warn Hartley that if he thinks he can carry on with this affair, he'd better think again."

"My husband has no intention of carrying on as before," Claire said, with bravura. "He has me to reckon with now!"

Jamie could not help but grin at the petite woman sitting beside him. "You?"

"Me," she said firmly.

Jamie looked as if he wanted to say something more, but before he could speak, dinner was announced and they made their way into the dining room. He was placed across the table from her, so they weren't able to continue any conversation which was a relief to Claire, though she found him staring at her several times throughout dinner. Afterwards, when they returned to the living room for coffee, the conversation remained general.

Later, when she left the room to get her coat, Jamie caught her in the hallway for a few moments. "Will you have lunch with me if I telephone you next week?"

Surprised by the request, Claire nodded and hurried upstairs without another word. She was slipping on her jacket when Miranda came up behind her.

"Claire, darling. I haven't had one minute to speak with you alone all evening."

"It's just as well," Claire said shortly. "I don't think we have anything to say to each other."

"Don't be so silly. Resentments aren't good for the heart and they weaken the soul. You aren't still blaming me for what I did, are you? After all, I really thought I was doing you a good turn. I certainly didn't force you to marry Hartley. You did that because you wanted the money."

It was a valid remark and Claire didn't respond to it. "None of us have come out of this little episode very well, I'm afraid, Miranda. But I don't think my reason for doing what I did was quite as unsavory as yours and Hartley's. I simply entered into a business opportunity."

Miranda sank down on the bed, her face uneasy and at that moment, Claire realized that the evening had not been easy for her. Loving Hartley must have made it difficult for her to see him with a wife, even if she knew the marriage was a contractual one.

"An impartial observer might observe that Hartley and I love Burnett even more than we love each other. Our concern for his health outweighed our own happiness."

"Then Hartley should have gone out of your life," Claire said curtly.

"He would have if there had been no other answer! Marrying you seemed to be the solution. You've got to admit it solved your problem too so don't stand there looking down on me. We're all on a dung heap and you do not come out of this smelling of roses!" Miranda forced a laugh. "I hate this. You've made me lose my temper and I try not to do that."

She smoothed a hand across her brow. "It gives me frown lines."

Claire walked towards the door. "I don't want to argue with you, Miranda. It's pointless and useless. But I don't want to be friends with you either."

"You don't want to be friends with me?" Miranda echoed. "Well, aren't you being the bitch! I'm the one who suggested one hundred thousand dollars as payment for marrying Hartley. That isn't an amount to be sneezed at!"

"I have no intention of collecting the other fifty thousand dollars."

"What? What's that supposed to mean? By the time your marriage is annulled, I'm sure you will have earned it." Miranda sounded panicked now.

"How will I have earned it?"

"Hartley isn't the easiest man in the world to live with. He isn't in love with you, so he's likely to be even more difficult – more distant."

"I haven't noticed him being difficult, so far," Claire said sweetly. "In fact, he's been quite the opposite – charming, attentive."

Miranda's eyes flashed with anger as she turned to face Claire. "Oh he's still on his best behavior with you, darling," she cooed. "Don't expect him to act the normal husband and I mean that in every way possible."

"Well, I shall be sure to send you an e-mail when he does," Claire snapped back.

"Oh, my," Miranda whispered. "I don't believe it! Don't tell me you've fallen in love with him, darling?"

"That's ridiculous!" Claire opened the bedroom door but Miranda was beside her in a flash, keeping pace with her as she walked down the corridor. "Why is it ridiculous, my pet? Hartley is very good looking and sexy."

"Just because you find him attractive, don't assume that every woman does."

"But you must find him handsome, no?"

"No!" Claire said, and then knowing that she sounded childish, corrected it. "Yes, of course I can see that he is handsome. But he is not my type. I prefer someone more like – well, like Jamie!"

Miranda laughed. "How funny would that be if you and Jamie fell for each other? It would give everyone a good, hearty laugh."

"Stop talking garbage, Miranda. Just let it go!" Claire went down the stairs ahead of her.

Hartley was waiting in the hall and Claire flung him a cold look before going back into the living room to say good night to Burnett, who was lying on a reclining chair.

"I'm sorry we stayed so late and kept you up, Burnett," she said, bending down to kiss him.

"Don't apologize, Claire. I regard you and Hartley as part of my family, and I'm quite relaxed with you. I only get tired when I'm with strangers." He squeezed her hand. "Come again soon. I always enjoy seeing you, my dear."

Sitting beside Hartley in the car, Claire wondered if he resented having her beside him instead of Miranda. But he made no reference to it and merely commended her on the way she had drawn Jamie out.

"He was chatting with you for a long time. I've never seen him so relaxed and comfortable with anyone. He's generally more nervous and unsure of himself."

"There's no reason why he should be."

"Well, he's overly ambitious. He wants to run before he can walk. If your ambitions outweigh your maturity, you either develop an inferiority complex or a superiority one."

"Thank you, Dr. Freud!"

He chuckled at her remark and turned a corner. Hartley handled the car with ease, just as he handled his whole life. No doubt he controlled all situations with which he had to deal.

"You know I'm right about Jamie," he continued. "He should have worked his way up from the bottom. Instead, he was brought into the company at the executive level. And if I mention it to him, he gets irritated and thinks I'm preventing him from receiving his promotion."

"I'm sure you would love it if he was no longer with the company."

"That's not true. My own feelings don't come into it at all. He certainly knows the workings of the company and his insight has merit. But, he's not a leader and he's not ready to take a directorship. That's my point."

Claire knew he was speaking the truth; knew that his ability to keep his personal feelings at bay was part of his strength. This enabled him to compartmentalize and to separate the mundane from the important, especially with his business transactions. He would also be able to keep his emotional life sealed off in precisely the same way. She wasn't able to do it; love would be her whole existence, she feared. It would color her thoughts and her actions, as her love for Hartley was doing right now.

"I don't blame Jamie for picturing himself in your shoes," she said. "After all, he is Burnett's only living relative."

"He's not one-tenth as capable as his uncle in business affairs. In ten years, he might make a good second-in-command, but never more than that. He should have stuck to architectural design, which is what he originally planned to do."

"Why did he change his mind?"

"Because Burnett fell ill and asked him to join the company. He felt it important for someone named Farber to carry on."

"But now he's happy for you to carry on?"

"Yes," Hartley said. "I'm lucky in my relationship with Burnett. That makes my love for Miranda all the more difficult."

"I'd rather not discuss that!"

He drove on for awhile before he spoke again. "It isn't like you to run away from the facts, Claire."

"I'm not running away from them. I just don't see the point in discussing them. I know how you and Miranda feel about each other. I know that when she's free, you will want to marry her. So, what is there to discuss?"

"If you put it that way, there's nothing more to talk about. But I don't feel that we can be completely honest with each other."

"Honest? Well, we have different ideas of what honesty is," Claire spat out.

"There you go, hitting below the belt again," he said curtly, and this time said no more until he had parked the car. "I'd like to start giving a few dinner parties. If you call my secretary tomorrow, she will give you a list of the people I wish to invite. There are about three dozen in all. If you can arrange five or six dinners, it shouldn't be too much for the housekeeper to manage."

"Are there any particular people you'd like me to invite?"

"Bernadette can tell you about that when she gives you the list. You won't go wrong if you take her advice." He hesitated. "It won't be too much for you to organize, will it?"

"Of course not. I was hoping to be busy with something. I was getting a bit bored, actually."

"Fine. Call Bernadette in the morning and we'll get started."

The next morning as Claire was discussing details with the housekeeper, she started to seriously doubt if the woman would be capable of organizing the dinners.

"I came here to work for Mr. Dale when he was a bachelor," she huffed. "And he said that there would be no entertaining at all."

"Well, we've changed our minds. He wishes to start inviting people over. Plans change."

"Those were not the terms on which I was hired. Mr. Dale knows …"

"Mr. Dale knows what he wants. If you don't wish to remain here under the new terms, then you had better find another position elsewhere." Claire stood still, waiting for the response.

"Are you giving me my notice?" the housekeeper said, clearly rattled.

"Yes." Claire knew she was doing the right thing. There was no point in having both a cook and housekeeper to cater to only two people. She needed to find someone else.

"How are you paid?"

"Weekly, madam."

"Fine. Then you may leave on Friday."

The housekeeper was angry. "You won't find someone else that easily. How will you manage?" She tried to appease Claire. "I'm willing to stay on if you hire a part-time cook to help me in the kitchen."

"No thanks. I prefer to find someone else."

Checking through the internet directory for domestic agencies, Claire knew it would not be all that easy to replace the housekeeper. But she made one call after another and, after her eighth call, had a stroke of luck. The agency had one person available who had contacted them just that morning. Her employer had died months before and she had decided to retire, but had found it so boring that she now wished to resume work.

"I can't give you any references at this time," the woman at the agency explained, "but she seems very pleasant and it would be worth your while to see her. Her name is Mary Winters and she lives in Flamborough which is near Waterdown."

"Mary Winters!" Claire could not hide her excitement. "She worked for Mr. and Mrs. Merton, a wealthy couple who lived very close to where I grew up. I'll take her immediately if she's willing to come to Toronto."

"Well, I'll call her and arrange an interview."

"There's no need. I'll go and see her myself. I know where she lives."

"Well, I think it would be better if I ..," the woman at the agency began.

"I'll pay your finder's fee, of course," Claire interrupted.

"Well, in that case, I'll leave you to make your own arrangements."

Determined to find Mary and hire her before someone else did, Claire decided to call for Hartley's chauffeur to drive her out to Flamborough immediately. She tried to call her home, but no one answered and there was no answering service. Changing into a warm winter coat, Claire arranged the driver and left the apartment within fifteen minutes.

It was strange to return to her home town after being away for more than a month. She went first to her house to check that everything was in order. In the past few weeks, Claire had changed so much that she was no longer sure that she could resume her life in a small town when the marriage was over. Once she was parted from Hartley, she had a feeling that she would want to move into the city where there was more excitement and action.

Locking up the house, she got back into the limousine and directed the driver to Mary Winter's small cottage. It looked as if it had been built to make a picture postcard. Instructing the driver to wait, she walked up the steps and knocked on the door. Mary, short and plump with grey hair pulled back into a neat bun, answered the door and her face broke into a huge grin when she saw Claire standing there.

"Why Claire. How delightful to see you. My, how beautiful you're grown. Come in." Mary invited her in and put the kettle on. Over a quick cup of tea, Claire explained her situation and Mary said that she had no hesitation in accepting the job. Though she had never lived in a penthouse in the big city, she was sure she could get used to it.

"The main thing is for me to be happy with the people I work for.

I've known you Claire for all your life. I had so many fine years with Dr. Merton and his family and felt at home. I think I would feel the same way with you and your husband."

"That's wonderful Mary. Just tell me when you can be ready to come to Toronto."

An hour later, Claire was on her way back to the city. All arrangements had been made and the chauffeur would be returning to collect Mary and her belongings on Saturday afternoon.

It was very late when Claire returned to the apartment. She hadn't counted on getting caught in rush-hour traffic. It was well past seven o'clock when she put her key in the door and, as she entered the front hall, Hartley strode out. He seemed angry and out of breath when he came up to her.

"Where have you been?" he spat out.

"I went to Flamborough today with one of your drivers."

"Without telling anyone? You could have left word with my secretary, or left me a note letting me know when you were returning."

"I expected to be home much earlier, but traffic was awful."

He followed her back into the living room and she looked back and studied his face.

"Is anything wrong?" she asked him. "Burnett isn't ill again?..."

"No, Burnett is all right," he said quietly. "I was worried about you. I thought you had an accident."

Surprise rendered her speechless. She was delighted that Hartley had been worried about her. It was incredible, but she didn't want to show any awareness. "I'm quite capable of looking after myself, Hartley," she said carefully.

"Maybe so, but you are my wife and I don't want you running around without letting me know where you are."

She giggled.

"What is so funny?" he asked.

"You are being a little over protective, don't you think?" She smiled.

If anything, he looked angrier. Just when she thought he was going to start yelling, he broke into a smile and suddenly seemed relaxed.

"Well, maybe I was being protective. But I did worry Claire."

She touched his arm reassuringly and then brought both arms together, hugging herself.

"You look cold and tired," he said, "Come to the fireplace and sit while I pour you a glass of wine."

Sipping on her red wine, she told him the story of the housekeeper and of finding Mary Winters. He looked quite relieved when she recounted her discovery of Mary's availability.

"Well, aren't you lucky? A good housekeeper who is also a good cook is difficult to find."

"It isn't just because she's an excellent cook that I'm so pleased. It's because she's kind and willing to do a hard day's work. That's so important. There's nothing worse than having someone around you who is resentful."

"How right you are!" he said.

His look was so keen that she knew he was referring to her own attitude to him. Because she was so honest, she didn't even pretend to misunderstand him. "I will always try my best to fulfill the bargain I made with you," she said. "If I do anything you don't like, please tell me."

"Thank you Claire. The same goes for me. Though I'm sure that if I do anything you don't like, you will have no hesitation in letting me know!"

"You made me sound like a big ogre," she sighed.

"No, only a very small one," he laughed. "I'm not making fun of your height, my love. You suit me very well just the way you are."

Claire thought about how nice the words 'my love' sounded. Wishing she really did suit him very well, she stood up. "I'm cold. I'm going to change into some warm pants and a big sweater and perhaps two pairs of socks!"

"Okay, but hurry. Dinner is waiting."

She quickly changed and rejoined him within moments in the dining room. His look indicated his appreciation of the black wool pants and soft pink sweater which lent color to her skin. Her cheeks still glowed from the cold air and they remained bright during the meal. It was the first time they had dined alone since their return from Paris. On most nights Hartley had either come home late – having already dined out with a business associate – or brought someone from the office home with him.

They chatted easily and then went back to sit by the fire, enjoying their coffee. "I've enjoyed this evening very much, Claire," he said. "I don't usually relax like this."

"So I've notice. Don't you ever get tired of working constantly?"

"Well, I get more tired when I don't. Work is my hobby."

"Don't you miss university life?"

"Yes, sometimes. But I know I wouldn't have the patience to remain there for long. I have inherited my liking for business from my mother's family."

"Do you ever see your relatives?"

"Yes, usually at Christmas. I have lots of cousins in Vancouver."

"Miranda's family comes from Vancouver." As Claire spoke, she wished she could take back the words, afraid that the mention of Miranda would make Hartley withdraw into his shell again. But if anything, he relaxed even more, for her words reminded him that it was through Miranda's family that he had first met Burnett.

"Yes, a cousin of Miranda's was a student of mine at the university," he said, "and he invited me to spend a weekend with him at his beach house. Well, Miranda and Burnett were there that same weekend and you know the rest."

"I don't actually. I only know that you suddenly went to Toronto to work for him."

Hartley rubbed his cheek and she noticed that he had a shadow of stubble on it. She wondered if his skin would be rough to the touch, and longed to put her fingers against his face. Forcing the thought away, she concentrated on what he was saying.

"Well, Burnett and I got along famously at that first meeting. He invited me to come to Toronto for a visit and we spent lots of time together. One evening over cocktails, he introduced me to a friend of his from the New York office. At dinner, another friend came to join us and he worked for Bantam Books. His name is Gregory

Harrison – do you know him?"

"Yes, I've heard of him."

"Harrison asked me to do a book about Toronto; to trace its history and the effect of its financial health upon the rest of the country's economy. That was a carrot in front of the donkey because in order to write the book, I had to learn much more about Toronto than I already knew, and the more I learned, the more fascinated I became with the business culture. The book was a great success and I was asked to follow it up with one about the six biggest investment firms in the country."

"And of course, Farber Investments International was one of the firms that you had to research," Claire added.

"Yup. All Burnett had to do after that was rope me in." His blue eyes narrowed. "He must have been very far-seeing to have recognized my business potential."

Far-seeing in business, but blind in matters of the heart, thought Claire bitterly.

"Well, no wonder Burnett feels so fatherly towards you. He is your Pygmalion."

"And I am yours," Hartley said as he leaned forward to touch her silky black hair, allowing his fingers to trace along her cheek down to her bottom lip. He let his fingers linger for a moment on her soft lip before drawing his hand back. "The change in you is quite remarkable, Claire."

"I'm the same woman you met," she said, breathlessly. "It's late Hartley. I'm going to bed. I feel exhausted.

"I'm not tired at all," he said. "You always seem to refresh me."

She stood there a moment longer, debating whether or not to return to sit beside him on the leather couch. Too moved to speak, she quickly turned and went into her bedroom.

His words remained with her for a long time as she lay in bed and stared out the window at the dark, stormy sky.

Chapter 10:

Claire entered the restaurant and look around. Several pairs of masculine eyes regarded her with interest. Finally she saw Jamie Farber sitting at a table near the window. He waved and smiled at her.

"I'm so glad you were able to come to lunch with me today," he said. "I hope you don't mind me asking you on such short notice."

"I was happy you asked me. It's broken up the boredom of the day."

"You don't look the type to be bored."

"I never thought I would be," she said, "but I've never lived the life of the idle rich until now." She took a quick look at the menu and then stared around the restaurant. "Look at everyone here enjoying themselves on their bloated business expense accounts. What a waste of time and money."

"More business gets done over lunch than in an office, Claire."

"Probably because more martinis and wine get drunk at the same time."

"My, aren't we cynical today!"

"Jamie, I don't mean to be. I'm just feeling resentful and bored. I really must find myself something useful to do."

"When you told me you were a social worker, I couldn't believe it. You look far too fragile and exotic to have worked in that field."

"Well, you should have seen me before I married Hartley. I wasn't quite so exotic-looking then."

"I don't believe that."

"It's true."

"Are you happy in your marriage?"

She had been expecting the question, but the bluntness of it took her by surprise. She looked down at her wedding ring. It was a circlet of diamonds, one of the most expensive things that Hartley had bought her.

"You haven't answered my question, Claire," Jamie said.

"What bride would ever admit to being unhappy?"

"You aren't a real bride."

"How do you know that? Would it be such a shock to learn that Hartley should genuinely like me?"

"You know I didn't mean that," he said. "Quite the opposite, in fact. But any man who is foolish enough to fall for Miranda..."

"You're speaking about a friend of mine."

"Is she still?"

"What do you mean?"

"It's obvious that Miranda drummed up this whole plan. She must have thought of you the minute she heard my ultimatum to Hartley. It was pretty clever of her. If you want to make sure of your lover, marry him off to your best friend."

The diamonds on Claire's finger winked with a thousand lights and she quickly blinked the tears from her eyes.

"Do you mind if we change the damn subject? I find it very unpleasant," she sighed.

"I'm sorry," Jamie looked genuinely concerned. "I assumed you wouldn't mind talking about it."

"Well, I do mind." She forced herself to pick up her knife and fork but it was an effort to eat the food. To Claire, it tasted like it was made of sawdust and she chewed and swallowed without any recollection of what it was she was eating. She was aware of Jamie looking at her with curiosity. Was he upset because he had hurt her feelings? It was obvious that his invitation to lunch was prompted by both curiosity and...something else - perhaps also by a desire to get to know her better? In an odd way, she felt that she was dining with a marriage broker because James Farber, more than anyone else, was responsible for her becoming Hartley's wife.

"Why are you smiling?" Jamie asked.

"I was thinking I have you to thank for my marriage."

"Well, if I had seen you first, Hartley wouldn't have had the chance."

"Why, Jamie. Are you flirting with me? Or is it my Paris hair-do that's bringing out this side of you?"

"I am not just being flip. I mean it, Claire." Jamie looked uncomfortable.

"You'd better put it down in writing."

"I intend to say it to you so often that it won't be necessary to write it down."

"Do you always talk to married women like this?"

"You are the first married woman I've ever taken out," Jamie said, then blushed. "Besides, I don't regard you as being properly married."

"Are you calling me improper?" she asked, then smiled.

He signaled for the waiter to clear their plates and replenish their wine glasses. "I don't see you marrying a man you don't love. On the other hand, you seem too smart to have been fooled by Hartley. Maybe you also had your reasons for getting married, hmm? I wonder what that reason could be?"

She smiled, but refused to answer Jamie on the subject. He could assume whatever he liked about her marriage but as long as she didn't answer his questions, he wouldn't know whether he was right. She didn't understand her reluctance to tell him the truth and wondered if it was a fear that, by doing so, she might lessen her chance of making Hartley fall in love with her. As long as she could pretend her marriage was real, perhaps it might eventually become so.

Hard on the heels of this thought came anger with herself. She would do far better to face the truth and accept Miranda's invincibility. No other woman could compete with such beauty and self-assurance. Wryly, she wondered what Hartley's friends would think if they knew the truth.

Since Mary Winters had come into their life a month ago, they had done a great deal of entertaining, and she knew that she and Hartley had given the impression of contentment and happiness. Sometimes as she looked at him, she wondered if it was all an act on *his* part, but she had never yet been able to find an answer to that question. Perhaps he could close his mind to the truth and believe what he wanted to. Maybe this was a performance which, had it been on film, would have earned him an Oscar nomination.

"Oh, God. There's Hartley," Jamie said. "He's just come in."

Claire turned quickly to see her husband threading his way between the tables to sit at one on the opposite side of the restaurant. His companion was an elderly man and they both looked very serious.

"It's Watson," Jamie explained. "He's been trying to wean Hartley away from Farber's for months."

"Hartley would never leave Burnett," Claire said firmly.

"He would have had to if he hadn't married you," Jamie said bluntly.

Claire watched Hartley as he studied the menu. His glance was brief – as if he had already decided what to eat and did not wish to waste time thinking about it – and he set the menu down and let his gaze move idly across the room. She knew he was not aware that they were here but was instantly able to tell when he spotted her. She saw his start of recognition and, even at a distance, could tell that his face had reddened upon seeing Jamie. Then he stood up, murmuring something to his luncheon companion, and wound his way through the tables towards her.

"I didn't know you were lunching here, Claire," he said.

"I didn't know either until mid-morning. Jamie telephoned me unexpectedly."

"Did he?" There was disbelief in Hartley's voice and animosity too. Somehow it didn't surprise her, for she knew he had little reason to like Jamie; unlike herself who was beginning to like him more and more.

"I hope you will both join us for coffee?" Hartley was speaking again, including Jamie in his invitation although he was looking directly at Claire.

Not sure what to do in this matter, Claire glanced over at Jamie and he nodded to her. "That would be very nice Hartley," she said. "Give us a nod when you've reached dessert and we'll come over and join you."

Hartley turned and went back to his table. Claire could tell from the set of his shoulders that he was far from pleased at seeing her here with Jamie. She forced herself not to read jealously into his reaction; more likely it was a possessive attitude at seeing her with another male.

"Now this is going to be fun – having coffee with Hartley," Jamie said, with a sarcastic edge to his voice. "I won't be able to have you all to myself."

"You're a very unsubtle luncheon date," she responded.

"And you are very blunt!"

"It's all part of my charm," she giggled.

"Actually it is, Claire. You're very candid and that's refreshing. People must have told you that before."

"Yes, I've heard it once or twice."

"Your smallness is part of your charm too."

"Let me guess. It makes all the men in my life feel like they're big and strong!" She clasped her little hands to her cheek.

"Probably."

"Well, that would be wrong," she answered. "All the men in my life merely look upon me as a good sport; a buddy."

"I don't believe it."

"It's true. All the men in my life have looked upon me with less than a romantic eye. That's why I enjoyed working for Miranda. Her life was romantic, glamorous, exciting. It gave me a glimpse of how the other half lived."

"And now you're the other half."

"I know," she paused. "But I still feel the same. Well, not quite. Knowing that you now look your best does wonders for your ego."

"I'm a good ego builder too!"

She widened her eyes at him and blinked her long, black lashes. "Are you purposely flirting with me, Jamie?"

"Do you object?" he asked.

"Not really. But you'll be wasting your time."

"I don't think so." Though he was still smiling, there was an intenseness in his face that was not humorous at all. "I plan to remain in your life, Claire – whenever you need a shoulder to cry on."

"Hartley will be delighted to learn that."

THE HIRED BRIDE

"I'm thinking of later; of the time when Hartley is no longer in your life." She refused to respond to him and turned to choose a piece of cheesecake from the dessert cart.

"For a slender woman, you sure knock back your food," he commented, gazing on the plate heaped with almond cheesecake and whipped cream which was set down before her.

"Everybody says that," she grinned and attacked her dessert with enthusiasm.

"Darn. I thought I was being original."

"Well, you're going to have to try harder. That also applies to your remark about being my dependable "cry on the shoulder" friend. That line has been around for decades!"

Jamie's features sharpened. "You never mince your words, do you Claire?"

"Part of my charm, remember?"

He laughed out loud.

She glanced over to where Hartley was gesturing with his hand for them to join his table. "Are you coming with me to join Hartley for coffee?"

Jamie sighed and nodded, then followed her as Claire rose and moved over to her husband's table. In Hartley's presence, she noticed that Jamie lost a bit of his puff and confidence. He was now very much the young man dining with his superior. But then, Claire noticed that Hartley made every man look insignificant in his presence. Smiling with charm, Claire chatted easily with both Hartley and his business associate.

"I do hope that you and Hartley will dine with me one evening?" Mr. Watson was looking in her direction. "Which evening would suit you best, Mrs. Dale?"

"You'd better ask my husband."

"Well, your wife is very diplomatic, Dale," he said, turning to Hartley.

"Or well-trained," he replied, grinning.

"I prefer the word diplomatic to well-trained," Claire retorted, and everyone laughed.

"I'm sorry darling," Hartley said, taking her hand. "It was only a joke and a bad one, I'm afraid."

At that, Jamie glanced at his watch and stood up. "I have an appointment at the office and must run. Please excuse me."

Immediately Claire stood up as well. Hartley frowned at her. "There's no need for you to leave too."

"Yes, I must," she smiled. "It's only polite since James was the one who brought me here. I'm sure you and Mr. Watson have a lot of business to discuss."

Hartley looked as though he was going to protest, but he didn't and leaned forward to kiss her lightly on the cheek. "I'll see you at home later, darling." This act was surprising to her, and she looked at him with wide eyes.

"You didn't have to leave with me, Claire," Jamie remarked as they climbed into a taxi.

"What do you mean? You were my luncheon date."

"Are you always so careful about watching your social etiquette?"

"I don't like hurting people's pride."

"Well, Miss Sharp Tongue – you could have surprised me!"

They both laughed easily. He took her hand in his, but she pulled it back immediately.

"Claire? Will you let me see you again?" he asked.

"Why?" He stared at her with such astonishment that she felt she had to explain her question. "I mean – are you taking me out because you know it will irritate Hartley; or because you genuinely enjoy spending time with me?"

Jamie blushed. "Annoying Hartley might have been the original reason. But it doesn't apply any more. It's you I'm interested in. As for offending Hartley – all I can say is that I wish he had never come into your life."

"Well then you would never have met me," she said.

"And that goes to prove that every cloud has a silver lining." He took her hand again and this time she didn't pull away. "I hope this cloud blows over soon, Claire even though it means my poor uncle…"

His voice trailed away and she realized that he understood their marriage would only last as long as Burnett was alive. Once his uncle died, then Hartley and Miranda would be free to marry.

"You really are very fond of your uncle, aren't you?" she asked quietly.

"Yes. My father died when I was nine years old and Uncle Burnett has looked after me ever since."

It was on the tip of her tongue to ask whether he felt that, by right of succession, he should be where Hartley was now. There was no way of asking this diplomatically, so she said no more until the taxi dropped her off outside of her apartment building.

"I guess you're always busy in the evening?" Jamie murmured as he walked her to the entrance.

"Even if I weren't, I wouldn't see you. It wouldn't be wise and it wouldn't feel right to me."

"Are you worried what people would say?"

"I would be worried what Hartley would say," she said.

"Would he even care?"

It was the most direct remark Jamie had made. "What new husband wouldn't care if his wife went out with another man?"

"Don't keep up the act with me," he said roughly. "I know damn well he only married you to keep his position with the company!"

"Goodbye Jamie," she said, and held out her hand to shake his. "Thank you for lunch."

He held onto her soft hand. "Claire, when can I see you again?"

She sighed and looked into his pale, young face. She pulled her hand away from his and turned to the open door, where the door man stood waiting for her to enter.

"Call me," she said, hurrying inside.

She was still not sure whether he was genuinely attracted to her – as he claimed – or if it stemmed from irritating Hartley. This brought her back to Hartley's behavior in the restaurant which, had she not known him better, she might have mistaken for true jealousy. It was dangerous to keep on thinking about it because her heart could give her false hope which would, eventually, lead to even greater unhappiness. She concentrated on the evening ahead. They were giving another dinner party and she went into the kitchen to check on everything.

As usual, Mrs. Winters had control over every detail; pots simmered gently on top of the stove and the silverware and china sat pristine and gleaming, ready to be set out on the dining room table. Knowing there was nothing to do except dress and make herself look pretty, Claire set out to do so. It was a pity her father couldn't see her now she mused as she opened her wardrobe and chose one of her many designer dresses. How pleased he would be by the luxury and beauty of her surroundings. Most importantly, he would have enjoyed Hartley's intelligence and success.Immediately, this made her wonder what Hartley saw in Miranda.

Just because a man was intelligent didn't mean that he wanted intelligence in the woman he loved. More often than not, he would settle for beauty alone. Not that Miranda was foolish or stupid, but she was not intelligent in the accepted sense of the word. She was cunning, based on her own preservation and the desire for financial security. This was her modus operandi.

The telephone rang and Claire picked it up. It was Miranda. She had to force herself not to slam it down.

"Why the hell haven't you been to visit me?" Miranda said, without preamble. "You're acting as if I was a stranger."

"You are."

"Don't be ridiculous. Just because I didn't tell you the whole story about Hartley."

"The whole story?" Claire exploded. "You told me nothing! If you were really a friend, you would have told me the truth and let me decide whether or not I wanted to get involved in your affair."

"I was afraid that if you knew the truth, you wouldn't help me."

"All the more reason for you not to have lied."

"Claire, darling. Try to be reasonable. Can't you see you were the ideal girl to marry Hartley? The one person I could trust to do the right thing when I'm free to – be with him?" Miranda's voice became softer. "Please, Claire. I miss you terribly. I thought it would be so nice to live close to each other. There are so many fun things we can do together. I'm giving a party next week and you are the only one who knows how I like the flowers done."

Claire could not help smiling. Miranda didn't miss having a friend; she missed having a social secretary and hoped she could still cajole her into doing it. "I don't need to earn any money now, Miranda, but I can certainly recommend a good agency where you can hire someone."

There was silence on the other end of the phone and Claire could visualize Miranda frowning, not sure whether to take offence or to pretend she had not understood the implication of the remark.

"Now you're being ridiculous!" Miranda said. "You are the only person who knows how I feel about Hartley, so you're the only one with whom I can relax. I'm surprised at you for letting your silly pride stop you from being friends with me."

"We were never friends, Miranda. You used me."

The pause this time was longer, and when Miranda spoke, her voice was no longer calm. "You are being very bitchy, Claire. Maybe it isn't pride you're suffering from but unrequited love!"

"You seem quite determined to prove that I'm in love with your boyfriend."

"That's the most obvious reason for you being so spiteful." There was an edge of temper to Miranda's voice that was very unattractive. If only Hartley could hear her now. "Perhaps you do want Hartley for yourself. That could explain why you are so angry with me. Because you know that you could never steal him away from me. That's the only explanation."

The receiver trembled in Claire's hand. She forced herself to remain calm; she must never let Miranda guess how right she was.

"Well, darling," Miranda purred, "aren't you going to deny what I've said?"

"I will when I can get my breath back since at the moment I'm just astonished at what you've said. Still, I suppose it's easier for you to believe I don't want to see you because I love Hartley rather than admit it's because I'm disgusted with you."

"Good try, Claire but it won't work. If your emotions weren't involved, then your pride wouldn't be hurt. You have obviously fallen for my lover!"

"If it makes you happy to think so, go ahead. Now, if you'll excuse me, I must go."

"Of course, darling," Miranda laughed. "Just remember you'll never get him no matter how hard you try! He's mine and he will forever remain mine!"

"Goodbye Miranda," Claire replied gently, and putting down the telephone, retreated to the quiet calm of her bedroom. Only here did she give way to anger, pacing the carpet and throwing pillows all over the room. She wished she had the chance to throttle Miranda or Hartley or, better still, both of them.

The sound of the front door closing told her that Hartley had come home. She glanced at her watch and realized it was time to change for dinner. Though she was not his wife in the true sense, she was still the hostess and needed to be ready and waiting to greet the guests.

She was dressed and perfumed and waiting in the living room a few moments before Hartley joined her. His chestnut hair was still damp and curly from the shower. It made him look more handsome than ever and she could well understand how Miranda had felt when she had realized that the only way to keep him was either to leave Burnett or to find him a hired bride. It would have taken great courage or great certainty of his love to have allowed him to leave the company and move on. He was not a man to be without female companionship for long and it was not surprising that Miranda had hit upon the idea of using her plain little school friend as a watchdog. Who would she have chosen if she hadn't known Claire? Some other little mouse, willing to play the part for the right price, she supposed.

Hartley wasn't a snob, but he certainly would never have married anyone who did not fit into his world. Yet, how did he evaluate her potential? They had barely spoken half a dozen sentences before he asked her if she were willing to enter into a business marriage with him. Had he done this because he recognized that she could be turned into a beautiful swan with a change of make-up, wardrobe, and a clever hairdresser?

"You seemed to be enjoying your lunch with Jamie today," he remarked as he fixed her a sparkling water, with fresh lime. "You never told me that you were meeting him."

"I told you, I didn't know it myself until he phoned me around ten o'clock."

"You went with him on short notice."

"And why not? My diary isn't crammed with engagements."

Hartley went back to the sideboard and poured himself a scotch-and-water. Holding it, he came to sit beside her. "From that remark, I take it you're bored?"

"I'm ready to climb the walls," she confessed. "I wanted to discuss with you my taking on a part-time job."

"Your job is to look after me," he said flatly.

"We have a housekeeper for that. And you have a secretary to take care of you at work."

"You know what I mean."

"I do, but you also know what I mean. You can't expect me to twiddle my thumbs around here all day."

"There are a lot of charities you can work for."

"Oh, joy; I can organize luncheons and bazaars with old matrons. Have a heart! You know I can do something more worthwhile than that."

"Isn't it worthwhile to be a wife?"

"To just be a wife? I don't think so," she began, "but then again, I wouldn't know because I'm not even a real wife – just a make-believe one."

His breath hissed out sharply between his teeth. "Yes, I wondered when you would be coming around to that point. At the risk of sounding repetitive, may I remind you that you are being paid well for this job? No one forced you to take on this position."

"I just don't see why I can't fulfill my part of the bargain, and still do some of my social work. It would be much more satisfying to me."

"What if I asked you to come away with me on a business trip? I frequently have to go away for a week at a time and it's often an advantage to have your wife along with you. We also entertain a lot here. I know you hired Mrs. Winters, but you do a lot of the organizing." He gently touched her face. "I don't want to be difficult, Claire. I just don't see how you can take on a part-time job without it affecting your life with me."

"Lots of women work and still manage to run their home – very well, and with no additional staff at all!"

"Yes, but they don't do the amount of entertaining that we do."

"You're making this difficult. You don't want your wife to work because of your position. It wouldn't auger well for me to be doing social work. That's the issue, isn't it?"

"Do you blame me?"

"Yes, I certainly do. If I were a doctor, or a lawyer, you wouldn't expect me to give up my career just because I married you."

"If you were a doctor or lawyer, I wouldn't have married you."

She stared at him. "You can't mean that!"

"I'm not sure," he said, softly.

Mrs. Winters came in with a small, exquisite basket of flowers; a group of tiger lilies surrounded by soft African violets. "For you, Mrs. Dale."

"How lovely!" she exclaimed, and even before she took out the card, she knew it was from Jamie.

"Both of these flowers remind me of you," he had written. "Thinking of you."

Aware of Hartley trying to read the card over her shoulder, she gave it to him and saw him look dour.

"I never knew Jamie was such a romantic," he said. "Be careful Claire. You don't know him very well."

"Are you warning me to stop my friendship with him?"

"Is it necessary for me to do so?"

She shrugged. "I don't know. But I probably see him in a different way than you. Frankly, I enjoyed his company today; he was amusing and very flattering."

"You sound like such a typical woman."

"Well, I thought you liked 'typical women'. After all, Miranda is such an obvious little piece of eye-candy."

She had never before made any sarcastic remark about Miranda and he gave her a sharp stare. But with a diplomacy that made her admire him, and dislike him at the same time, he went over to the sideboard to add more ice to his drink and changed the subject. He started telling her of the background of some of the guests attending tonight's dinner.

Claire pretended to be listening to him, but she was busy speculating on why he was so reluctant for her to continue seeing Jamie. For his part, Hartley didn't understand his feelings either. All he knew was that he was irritated at seeing Claire and Jamie together in the restaurant that afternoon. Throughout his meal, he had been watching her surreptitiously, his irritation turning to anger when he saw how much she was enjoying herself. She frequently threw back her head in laughter – the warm, uninhibited laugh that he always associated with her. When she and Jamie had joined him for coffee, there had been a sparkle in her eyes that had angered him even more.

Yet, why shouldn't she enjoy herself in another man's company? On her own admission she had not had much dating experience in her life. If finding that she had turned into a swan, from a plain duckling, had gone slightly to her head, who could blame her?

Over the rim of his glass, he surveyed her. Claire had never been an ugly ducking, not to anyone with the intelligence to see beneath her dull clothes and badly styled hair. But like the flowers that had been sent, she had blossomed over the past few months. He watched as she went to the window to pull the curtain into place. Her beauty was far from delicate now; exotic was a much better word to describe her alabaster skin and jet black hair. Her eyes were framed by amazing thick black lashes. If Miranda had known how attractive her friend would become, he was sure that someone else would have been chosen for him.

A picture of Miranda flashed into his mind. She was blank with astonishment at the sight of Claire upon her return from Paris. He had seen Claire's change as a metamorphosis, but Miranda's surprise would have been different. He could almost see anger in her face that day; and fear too. Surely Miranda knew she had nothing to fear from any other woman – especially not Claire.

Hartley thought that Claire's future lay with someone like Jamie. No, damn it – not Jamie – he was not good enough for her. He frowned in thought, trying to come up with a name of a young man for her – someone who would be worthy of being her husband. None of them, he decided; not one of them was worthy.

The arrival of the first guest brought him back from his reverie. He found himself thinking about Miranda again as he watched Claire gliding around the room, making everyone feel at ease. For someone who done little social entertaining, she had developed it into a fine art and seemed to have a natural gift for it. Even his old friend Percy Carmichael had actually been smiling.

He walked over to Claire and put his arm lightly around her shoulders. She trembled slightly at his touch and he gave her a firm hug.

"I'm not going to hurt you. I just came over to compliment you on getting Carmichael to smile."

Claire looked up at him. Her cheeks were flushed. "Doesn't he usually smile?"

"I don't think I've ever seen it. What on earth did you say to him?"

"I really can't remember. Something nice, I suppose."

He laughed. "Dear Claire! You always seem to say nice things to people. I suppose that's why they like you."

"I must remember that the next time I talk to you."

"I like you anyway."

"Do you?" There was a curious look in her eyes that he could not figure out.

"Of course," he answered, in surprise. "Didn't you know that? I like you very much." He felt annoyed when someone came up to speak to him before she could answer. But, as he turned away, he vowed to continue their conversation when they were alone together.

It was almost one o'clock before the final guest left and Claire, still energetic, went around gathering up glasses.

"Leave it for the maid, Claire. Sit down with me and relax."

"I hate to leave empty glasses around the living room. It makes the room smell of old wine and whiskey the next morning. Let me just gather up this tray and take them into the kitchen."

"Alright. Then come back and talk to me for a few minutes."

She nodded and, balancing the tray, left the room to go into the kitchen. As she did, the telephone rang and, wondering who could be calling so late, Hartley lifted the receiver.

It was Miranda, her voice high and breathless. "Hartley! Oh my God, it's Burnett." He didn't need her to go on, but she did and he listened intently. She rambled on, in shock, probably not knowing all that she was saying.

So, it had finally happened and when he least expected it.

"I'll be right over. Try to keep calm Miranda," he said quietly and was replacing the receiver when Claire came back into the room, her look questioning who was on the phone at this hour.

"It's Miranda." His voice was so low and thick with emotion that it surprised her. He cleared his throat. "Burnett had a massive heart attack earlier this evening. He died about half an hour ago."

"Oh no! Poor Burnett," Claire said, feeling her eyes welling up. "If only you had been with him."

"No. In a way, I'm glad that I wasn't."

She looked at him but he didn't explain what he meant but was sure that she understood. Even in her sorrow, she was glad that Hartley seemed to have integrity enough to feel guilty. How could he have been there at Burnett's side to watch him dying, knowing that with his death Miranda would now be free to be his?

The thought hit her like a slap and she had to grab onto the chair to steady herself.

"I ...said that I would go over to see Miranda," Hartley said slowly. "Do you want to come with me?"

"Why should I?"

"You were – you are her friend."

"She'll have you to comfort her, Hartley," she said coldly. "She won't need anyone else."

Hartley stood there and looked at her for a long time. "Don't wait up for me, Claire. I have no idea what time I'll be back. Good night."

And with that he grabbed his overcoat and left, locking the door behind him.

Chapter 11:

When Hartley left, she remained awake through most of the night. When dawn came, she had still not reached a decision as to what she should do now that poor Burnett was gone. Claire had always known that her marriage would end when Miranda was free, but she had never envisioned it happening so quickly. Logically, she knew that there was no longer any reason for her to remain here. The sooner their marriage was annulled the better it would be for her. Now that the time had come, she dreaded ending it.

"Get ready, Claire Dale," she said aloud, but quickly had to correct her name back to Claire Evans. She must think of herself as a single woman again. It would be prudent to take actions to resume her old life and her old job. She had been away from it for such a short time, she was sure it was still available for her. But, she knew instinctively that, though she could return to her life as it was before, it would never be the same again.

She forced herself out of bed and hopped into the shower then quickly got dressed. As she was having her breakfast, she heard the front door open. Hartley came in, looking peaked and exhausted and she could tell that he had not had an easy night of it. His face looked strained and tired and there was dark stubble on his chin which made him look older, the way he would look when he was in his mid-forties. "I won't be seeing him then" she thought sadly, and felt the sting of tears in her eyes. Quickly pouring him a cup of hot coffee, she set it down in front of him. He smiled his thanks and drank half of it before he spoke.

"The funeral will be at the end of the week. There will be a lot of people flying in from all over North America, the U.K. and Europe to attend."

"It was very sudden, wasn't it?"

He looked at her in surprise. "Not really, Claire. It's been expected for more almost two years."

"But he did show a slight improvement in the past few months."

Hartley nodded. "He had been having some new kind of treatment and was told that, if he took things carefully, he could possibly go on for years."

"But now he's gone and everything has changed for you." She had an intense desire to know the worst; to hear it from Hartley's mouth. Not that she didn't already know the truth - she just needed to hear it said out loud. But he didn't respond to her. Instead, he banged his cup sharply on the saucer and stood up.

"I'm going to shower and change. You must appreciate that there will be quite a lot for me to take care of – arrangements to make."

"Why can't Jamie do it? He was Burnett's nephew."

"Miranda would prefer that I did it. You don't seem to realize what a shock this had been to her."

"Shock? A relief as well, I would think," Claire said bluntly. Hartley looked at her with disapproval and anger.

"I'm surprised at your complete lack of empathy, Claire! For God's sake, Miranda was Burnett's wife for more than seven years!"

"She was also involved with you for the last two of them! Please, spare me any tired old clichés about bereaved widows!"

"Miranda loved Burnett! Maybe it was no longer in a sexual way, but it was a strong love – as if she were his daughter. If she had met me before Burnett became ill, she would have been able to leave him. By the time we did meet, it was too late and she felt obligated to stay because of his poor health. At least you can commend her for playing fair with her husband."

"Fair? I commend her for playing a waiting game," Claire retorted. "You're a fool, Hartley! Miranda didn't stay with Burnett because he was ill. She married him for his money and that's the reason she stayed with him. If she had left, she would have received a mere pittance of what she will now inherit as the 'widow Farber'. Are you so blind that you can't see? Miranda won the jackpot; she gets the Farber fortune and you as her handsome lover. What a great deal!"

"I'm surprised. That is the sort of remark I would expect from one of Miranda's enemies, not her good friend."

"I am not Miranda's friend!"

"What happened to all the charity and kindness you usually show to people, Claire?" His blue eyes flashed brightly as though they were filled with chips of ice.

"I don't believe that this situation merits charity or kindness. You and Miranda have finally got what you've waited for. You have your big, important position at Farber and now you also get Burnett's wife in the bargain. She has you, plus she has Burnett's money. You both should be feeling very pleased with yourselves right now. At the risk of offending, I would say you two deserve each other!"

Angrily, he turned and stomped out of the room, banging his bedroom door behind him.

Claire did not see Hartley again before he left the penthouse. She had been invited to attend a private viewing at a downtown art gallery, but didn't have the heart to go. Instead she put on a heavy coat and walked along the lake for a long time. Here she was away from the noise of the traffic and smell of the fumes. Suddenly she felt homesick. How silly it must have been for her to consider staying on in the city after the marriage was dissolved. She now knew that she would return to the small town she called home and resume her old job. Among friends, it would be much easier to stop fantasizing about a future that would never be hers.

Walking back towards the condominium, she felt that it would be socially correct to go and visit Miranda. But she just couldn't sympathize with her when she knew that Burnett's death had been looked forward to with relief.

On a grey, sodden day in March, Burnett Farber was laid to rest with hundreds of people attending to pay him last respects. Miranda, in black silk with a scarf of black chiffon covering her copper and gold hair, wept openly. She had never looked lovelier. It also happened to be exactly four months to the day since Claire and Hartley's wedding day. That small fact was probably lost on everyone, except for Claire.

Claire's glanced over to her husband, tall and quiet standing beside her, his dark curls ruffled by the cold wind. She closed her eyes and stood in silent prayer. She was startled when her arm was taken by Jamie, who guided her past the line of black limousines to his BMW. Hartley, as befitted his position as senior officer of Burnett's company, was guiding the widow Farber away from the grave and she clung to him, the very picture of bereaved widowhood.

"I'm driving you back to the house," Jamie murmured. "Hartley will be taking Miranda."

Claire nodded, grateful to not have to face Burnett's other relatives or business acquaintances, and she breathed a sigh of relief when they left the cemetery.

"What's going to happen with you now, Claire?" Jamie asked her. She looked over at him in his impeccable, dark Italian suit, and his brand new, fully-loaded BMW and realized that, for all his youth, Jamie was a wealthy man and likely to be much wealthier now that his uncle was dead.

"What do you mean?" she asked dully.

"Well, you won't be staying on with Hartley now that Miranda is free, will you?"

"I haven't thought that far ahead. I was more concerned with showing my respects to Burnett today," she answered coldly.

Jamie laughed, but without humor in his voice. "It isn't that far ahead Claire. It's here and now. You can't run away from the truth. I always thought you were a girl who liked to face the facts."

"Not the disturbing ones."

"You're the one who's making them disturbing. I'm trying to put them in order for you."

"Well, thank you!"

They drove on for several minutes and her anger slowly began to abate. Jamie was right. To deny it was futile. After all, he was only saying to her what she had said to Hartley. But, what would his reaction be if he found out that she had received money for becoming Hartley's wife? And there was another fifty thousand dollars to come on the day that their marriage was officially annulled?

She didn't take the time to think about his reaction. Speaking slowly, she told Jamie the whole story, covering everything from the conversation with Miranda until today's funeral.

He drove on for a long time in silence. "I assumed it was something like that, Claire. I'd had no idea that it was so much money. Hell, he can afford it and he'll get the money back a thousand times over now."

"You might not like Hartley," she protested, "but he wasn't in this deal for the money. He wants to marry Miranda because he's in love with her, not for her wealth."

"Oh, he won't be needing Miranda's money," Jamie answered. "Being with Farber Investments has given him plenty of his own. And now that he will be the chairman, he's got stock options, and annual bonuses worth enough to feed a third world country."

"When you gave him the ultimatum, did you hope that he would resign and leave you to step into his shoes?"

"I'm not going to take offence at that remark," Jamie said calmly, "because I know that you're upset and angry. But I had no desire, at any time, to step into Hartley's shoes – in his business or personal life. Until now."

"What do you mean?"

"I'm making no bones about my feelings, Claire. I've fallen in love with you and I want to marry you."

"Don't say that!" She burst into tears. "You make it sound as if everyone is glad that Burnett is dead. It's as if his dying was the best thing that could have happened to his family."

"You know very well how much I loved my uncle," he said. "The only reason I feel relief at his death is because I've always been afraid that one day he would discover what a bitch he'd married!" He drove faster and she started to get concerned at how much the car was speeding.

She lowered her eyes and nodded, agreeing with him. Within five minutes, they had reached Burnett's house. It's Miranda's house now, she thought, as she gave her coat to the hired butler. She had no intention of going upstairs to leave it in Miranda's room as she had so many times before. Those days were over.

Following Jamie into the dining room, she noticed that a buffet table had been set up and several servants, also hired for the day, were dispensing food and drinks. She shivered, wishing that she didn't have to face another hour of forced conversation with these people.

"When am I going to see you again?" Jamie asked softly, close to her ear.

She was about to reply when Hartley and Miranda entered the room. Even in fake grief, she looked gorgeous. She taken off her hat and coat and her simple black dress clung to every line of her tall, graceful figure. She held onto Hartley's arm and he was forced to move around beside her as she went from group to group. Did other people realize what a handsome couple they made? Was this Miranda's way of deliberately giving indication that this was the way it was going to be in future? How soon would she be planning to marry Hartley? Would she obey convention and wait for at least a year, or would she ignore what people might say and marry him the moment he was free? She couldn't shut her brain down to stop all these questions.

Either way, it didn't matter for she had no intention of standing by to wait while they made up their mind on how they were going to play this hand. She had helped them but now it was time to move on.

"Jamie, will you drive me home?" she asked. "My home. My house in Waterdown. Will you drive me there tonight?"

He was surprised, but nodded. "Of course. When do you want to leave?"

"In a few moments. But let's be discreet. When you see me slip out, leave a few minutes later."

"Well, I might not see you if I get involved in conversation, but..." Jamie's narrow face was tender as he looked down at Claire, who seemed so fragile and vulnerable. "Let's meet in exactly fifteen minutes at my car."

"Fine."

She was glad to have made a firm arrangement with him, for he was whisked away by an elderly man who spoke with a clipped British accent. The living room was so full of people that she had lost sight of Miranda and Hartley. She began to edge toward the door but all of the directors of Farber Investments were there with their wives and since most of them knew her, they took the opportunity to chat. This slowed her progress down considerably. At last, she escaped into the hall and hurried to the small room adjacent to the ladies washroom to retrieve her coat. The coats weren't there. They had moved them upstairs so she now had to run up to Miranda's bedroom to find hers.

She found the coat – the one that Hartley had given her on their wedding day – and slipped it on, sighing. Bending down to pick up her handbag, she saw Miranda and Hartley come into the room. Remembering the last time they had all been in Miranda's room and Claire had seen them in their passionate embrace, she turned quickly to exit.

"I'm just leaving, so you'll be quite alone in here," she told them.

"We don't have to worry about sneaking a moment like that anymore," Miranda said glibly. "Hartley only came up here to get a letter that Burnett had left for him." She walked over to her dressing table and took out a sealed envelope from the top drawer. Hartley slit it open and took out a single sheet of writing paper. It took him a moment to read it and watching him, Claire saw his eyes grow damp with tears and his lids blink rapidly.

"It's a personal goodbye from him," he said huskily, clearing his throat and refolding the letter.

"Did he say anything about us?" Miranda asked.

"Only that he hopes that I will – that I should always take good care of you."

"Then he never suspected a thing." There was satisfaction in Miranda's voice and she sank on to the bed. "Oh, Hartley, I'm so glad we did the right thing. We would never have known real happiness if we had been responsible for his death. But this way, we can happy together and not feel any guilt at all."

"Please excuse me," Claire said loudly, and went to the door.

"Wait. You can't leave. We have things to discuss," Miranda called to her.

"You don't need me here for that, Miranda."

"Of course we do. You're still Hartley's wife and we must decide how best to end it."

"Can't that wait for the moment?" said Hartley curtly.

"What is there to wait for, darling?" Miranda demanded. "Your reason for marrying Claire is over. The quicker you're free of her, the better for us."

Claire couldn't believe the bluntness of her words. Here now was the answer to the question she had asked herself downstairs. Miranda obviously intended to ignore convention and acknowledge her love for Hartley the moment she could do it.

"Miranda, please," he protested. "I prefer to discuss this another time."

"Don't be silly, Hartley," Miranda said. "It's ridiculous for us to pretend don't you think? She turned to look at Claire. "You must be very pleased that this is over so soon. This has to be the easiest hundred thousand dollars you'll ever earn in your life!"

"For heaven's sake, Miranda!" Hartley exploded. "There is no need to be rude!"

"Since when do you regard honesty as rudeness?" Miranda said, with a little laugh. "I'm sure Claire appreciates honesty, don't you pet?"

"Maybe she does," Hartley replied. "But there is no need to have this discussion here and now. Let it wait for …"

"There's no point in waiting," Claire said. "The quicker I'm rid of the both of you, the better!" She turned around to face Miranda. "It might be your ambition to become Mrs. Hartley Dale as quickly as possible, but remember, I'm just as eager to give up the title!" She opened the door and ran down the corridor, wondering if Hartley would come after her, but feeling no surprise when he didn't.

Hartley watched Claire go with an emotion that he could not name. His heart felt too big for his chest. It was too new, too strange. He didn't know what he was feeling. But he did know that he was furious with Miranda!

"Did you have to talk to Claire like that?" he said, closing the door and coming back towards the bed.

"What was wrong with what I said? She's been expecting to hear it. She knows that the end of the marriage is inevitable." Miranda stared at Hartley. "Frankly, darling, I'm surprised you didn't say to her already."

"With Burnett just dead?" He had occasionally been confronted with women who seemed to have ice water running through their veins, but nothing compared with the way Miranda was acting. It was surprising to him. She had always been so gentle and soft and vulnerable. He tried to put out of his mind the rude and matter-of-fact way that she had laid out their future, seemingly giving no thought to the man whom she had just laid to rest; a man who had been her devoted husband for more than seven years. This was a man whose love she accepted and whose money she now…He stopped, horrified at where his thoughts were taking him. Damn Claire and her insidious comments! Yet, he couldn't forget the things she had pointed out to him about Miranda. Suddenly all those comments seemed to flow into his head. He didn't like the woman he saw before him.

"It would have been more diplomatic if you had allowed me to speak to Claire," he said aloud.

"Since when do I have to be careful with what I say to her?" Miranda came towards him. "I'm free of Burnett, and I want to be with you. We don't have to pretend anymore. Isn't that wonderful, Hartley? We needn't hide our love!" She went to put her arms around him, but he moved away slightly, unconsciously. He only realized that he had moved away when he saw her drop her arms to her sides.

"I never wanted to hide our love, Miranda," he replied. "You are the one who wanted to do that."

"But you know why."

"I was just thinking. When I first asked you come away with me, the very first time, Burnett wasn't ill."

Miranda's delicate features sharpened as she frowned. "Why are we talking about the past? We should be planning for our future."

"Well, then we should think carefully." Hartley heard himself speak. Why did he suddenly feel so hesitant about planning his future with Miranda? If was as if he were seeing her for the first time, though a mist. No, not a mist; that was the wrong word. It's as if he was seeing her clearly, but she was blurred now because the new image was out of focus with the one he had always carried in his heart.

He stared at her oval face; at the smooth skin, the delicately featured cheekbones, and the large blue eyes that were watching him carefully. She was physically the most beautiful woman he had ever seen. Even looking at her now, he could appreciate that. Yet, there was some fundamental flaw in her personality that prevented the beauty from taking on warmth and texture. He put a hand to his forehead, and it came away damp.

"Hartley, darling. Are you ill?" Miranda came closer to him, her perfume making his senses swim the way it always did.

"I have a headache," he murmured. "I haven't eaten anything since breakfast."

"Oh my sweet," she said as she put her arms around him. "People will start to leave soon and then I'll ask them to make a special meal for you. Or would you like to have it sent up here now?"

"No, thanks. I don't think I could stomach any food." He moved back a step, but Miranda's arms stayed around him. Automatically he held her and she gave a small sigh and relaxed into him.

"I feel so calm with you," she said, as she gave another murmur of contentment. "I love you so much."

Hartley rested his cheek on her soft hair, feeling it rub against his cheek like a swatch of silk. How many times had he dreamed of the moment when he could hold Miranda in his arms and know there was no other man to come between them.

But now that Burnett was gone, Claire had taken his place as the one who came between him and Miranda. This was a perplexing situation for Hartley.

"We can't stay up here any longer," he said quietly and took Miranda's arms away from around him. "We must go back downstairs or everyone will be wondering where we are."

"They'll think I wasn't feeling well and that you came up to sit with me."

She put her arms around him again and pulled his head down for a kiss. As his mouth lay upon hers, her body pressed close and Hartley could feel her breasts swell against his chest. It had been several weeks since he held Miranda close and he was disconcerted by the lack of physical response he experienced. Perhaps he was ill – or work had tired him out? Certainly he could never remember a time when he had held Miranda in his arms and not wanted to make love to her. Again, he disengaged her arms from around him.

"We must go downstairs."

With grace, she accepted his suggestion and walked beside him along the corridor. He knew they made a striking couple. As well, he was aware that had he not been so recently married, many people in the living room would have already started to pair them together. Perhaps some still did. He and Miranda had been able to fool Burnett, possibly because Burnett chose to show a blind eye to them, but others would not have been able to judge the situation in quite the same fashion.

"I need to go home. I want to discuss things with Claire," he whispered as they reached the hall.

"Will you come back to me this evening?"

He hesitated and then shrugged, "I don't know. You'll have to give me some time." He was unwilling to make a definite commitment to Miranda. He didn't know why and the reason became more obscure as he drove through busy traffic downtown to his penthouse apartment. In his front hall, he stopped in surprise as he saw the pile of luggage. Who on earth had come to visit them? There were four large suitcases in all; all new and expensive and – he recognized the Viutton label – initialed with the letters "C.D." Was Claire walking out on him?

"Claire," he called. "Where are you?"

There was no answer and he strode quickly down the hall to Claire's room at the far end. Even as he pushed open the door, he realized it was the first time he had been in here, and the thought struck him as bizarre.

Claire was bent over a smaller case on the bed and she looked up blankly as he came in.

"Why didn't you answer me?" he demanded.

She shrugged and went on packing, not saying a word.

"Stop packing. Leave those things," he said harshly, and walking over, he banged the suitcase shut, narrowly avoiding her fingers. "Leave it," he repeated, "and answer me!"

"I have nothing to say."

"Do you mind telling me just where you're going?"

"I'm going home. I am obeying Miranda's orders and I'm leaving you."

"Miranda doesn't give you orders."

"You tell her that."

"I'm telling you that Miranda cannot tell you what to do!"

The look she gave him was wary, as if she was not sure what he meant by that. Well, how could she know when he really didn't know himself?

"Hartley," Claire said calmly. "The reason that we were married no longer exists." He forced himself to listen as she spoke, wondering for the second time in an hour what was wrong with him. Only a short time ago, he had the feeling he was seeing Miranda for the first time, and now he was experiencing the same thing with Claire. He closed and opened his eyes. It was even stranger than that for he wasn't just seeing one Claire, but a hundred images of her, each one on top of the other until he felt that he was in the centre of a kaleidoscope. Claire on the day he married her; Claire in Paris; walking into the restaurant with her new hair gleaming and her beautiful, exotic eyes; Claire smiling and then pensive; intelligent one moment and then argumentative the next.

Vividly he remembered their brief but happy stay in Paris when, for some reason, he had felt free and calm and younger than he had in years - light-hearted too, as if his honeymoon had been a genuine one and Claire was the wife he had wanted to share it with. He felt that he had grown to know her during those days, but that feeling had faded in the months since their return. Today, it felt that she was almost a stranger to him. Not quite a stranger because he could still remember the sensation of her lips upon his when he had kissed her;

and the feeling and scent of her skin when he had almost made love to her in Paris.

"Miranda is right, Hartley," Claire continued. "There's no longer any reason for us to remain married. The sooner we get it annulled, the better."

"What will you do?" he asked.

"I have my home and I'm sure I can get my job back."

"You seem very anxious to leave me!"

"I have my own life to lead. It's time to move on."

The door behind Hartley opened, and Jamie said. "Shall I start taking your luggage downstairs, Claire?"

"What the hell?" Hartley swung around and looked at the younger man. "Who gave you the right to take Claire away from me?" Only as he saw the look of comical surprise on Jamie's face did Hartley realize the ludicrous question he had asked. With an enormous effort of will, he forced himself to speak in an imitation of his normal, soft-spoken manner. "What I meant to say is that if Claire decides she wants to leave, I am perfectly capable of taking her wherever she wishes to go. I suggest you say goodbye and leave."

Jamie looked past Hartley to Claire who was still standing by the bed. Hartley knew she must have nodded because Jamie looked back at him and shrugged. "Claire wanted to go back home, and I offered to drive her."

"You're quite the little Boy Scout, aren't you James?" Hartley deliberately put the humor back into his voice, glad to see that it did the trick and Jamie blushed.

"Claire's life has been lacking in boy scouts, I would say," Jamie replied. "But I am more than willing to make up for that deficiency."

"Be careful what you say, pal," Hartley said quietly, "or I will have to give *you* an ultimatum."

Jamie ignored him and spoke directly to Claire. "You know where to find me if you need me."

"Yes, Jamie, thank you," she said breathlessly. "You'd better go now. I'll see you to the door." She took a step forward but Hartley put his hand on her arm firmly.

"He can find his own way out," he said softly. "Good night Jamie. I'll see you in the office in the morning." Hartley waited until he heard the front door click shut and then said. "Sit down, please Claire. It's been a trying day for you."

Gently, he shepherded her to a chair and pushed her into it. The bones of her shoulders felt tiny beneath his hands and he had to restrain the urge to hold her by the shoulders and pull her towards him in an embrace.She sat down and tilted her head up to look at him. Her eyes were so beautiful and they gazed at him fearlessly and with contempt. Well, why shouldn't they? He had done nothing to deserve anything else from her.

Their brief time together flashed through his mind like a slide show; the reason for their marriage; the unsavory reason for the annulment of it and all the events that lay between. The evenings that he had spent with Miranda when Claire had been left here alone; the dinner parties where she had acted as his hostess and he had treated her as if she was only hired help. She had been efficient at running his home, had been available whenever he needed someone to talk to – and how bright and receptive she was – and her ability to become invisible when she was not required.

He had taken all this for granted and, even worse, had considered it his right to do so. Yet, alongside this, another feeling had grown within him. Subtly, it had caught up with him. He was a fool because he had been too blind to see it. He clenched his hands tightly. The past was dead. His relationship with Miranda was over. But, unless he could convince Claire that this was the truth, his future would be dead too.

I love her, he thought.

The words came into his mind so simply and gently that it was like a kitten lapping at a saucer of milk. With the same insidiousness, it permeated his consciousness, turning his entire world into an empty space only she could fill.

It was not the burning passion he had always known with Miranda but something richer, deeper, more varied; compounded of desire and laughter as well as understanding and compassion. It was a feeling that would be with him for the rest of his life, he knew.

Carefully he sat down opposite her. He had to let her know, but didn't know where to begin. How could he tell her he loved her and expect her to believe him when all of his actions had pointed to the opposite? No, he dared not admit his feelings yet; he had to bide his time and show her without words. He thought of Jamie's eagerness to driver her away from him and suddenly felt a violent urge to smash his face. No one was going to take Claire away from him.

"Why are you looking at me like that?" she burst out.

"Like what?" he blinked.

"Like I'm a stranger."

"You are. We are all strangers to each other, I guess."

"Don't be maudlin," she said, bluntly. "It doesn't become you."

"Oh, you're back in form, I see!"

She smiled and shifted around in the chair. His eyes moved up her slender legs to the rounded curve of her hips and he thought, she's not a little girl; very much a woman. He looked at the curve of her breasts and suddenly felt a stirring in his body that he didn't experience with Miranda holding him closely. There was no doubt about his feelings. He had to gain control because all he wanted to do was pull her into her arms, kiss her deeply and carry him to bed with him.

"If you don't want Jamie to drive me to my home," she said. "Perhaps you'll be good enough to call the chauffeur to take me?"

"This *is* your home," he said. "You can't leave now. We've only been married a few months."

"I don't expect you to pay me the other fifty thousand dollars," she said, baffling him into silence. "I really know you expected me to act the part of your wife for a much longer period of time. To pay me such a large sum of money for only a few months work is unnecessary. So, we can just say that you've paid me in full and..."

"Money is the last think in the world that I'm thinking of!" he interrupted.

"Then what are you worried about? What people will say if I leave you so soon after our wedding?"

She had given him the lead he wanted, and he took it. "Yes. Since the whole purpose of our marriage was to avoid any gossip about myself and Miranda, it would rather spoil the effect if we rushed into each other's arms the moment that Burnett is dead."

"Miranda wants me to go immediately."

He longed to say that he didn't give a damn what Miranda wanted, and forcibly held himself in check. So many things were becoming clear to him that he knew how a blind man must feel when, through a medical cure, he regained his sight. Was this why Miranda had not wanted him to leave the company and try to make another life for himself? Had she feared that if he was away from her, he would see her for what she really was; a spoiled and selfish beauty who wanted to have it all? He glanced over at Claire and knew that no matter where he was and with whom he worked, this lovely dark-haired creature would always haunt him.

"Miranda made herself very clear, Hartley. She wants me to go."

"She wasn't thinking clearly," he replied. "Once she does, she will agree that my idea is the best."

"I can't stay here with you." Claire jumped to her feet and resumed her packing. "You needn't start the annulment yet if you don't want to, but I think it would be better if I moved out and went back to my own house."

"I won't let you," Hartley's voice was harsher than he had intended, and he saw the doubt on her face as she turned to look at him. "We made a bargain," he went on, "and I insist that you stick to it."

"Well, you can't make me stay – not if I'm willing to forfeit the other fifty thousand dollars."

"I'm not prepared to let you forfeit that money. Unless I agree to alter our agreement, it still stands. Of course, if you insist on breaking it…"

"I do," she said.

"Then you have to return the first fifty thousand dollars."

"Hartley! You know I can't do that," she spat out. "I've already given that money to Charles."

"Ah, yes." Mention of Charles gave Hartley another stab of jealousy and, unaccustomed to such an emotion, he blurted out the first thing that came to him, "Does your Jamie know about Charles?"

"You must know that I'm not in love with Jamie!" she said quickly. "I like him, that's all. He's been a friend to me."

"He intends to change all that, Claire."

"He might just succeed, Hartley!"

Claire's retort caused Hartley to hiss through his teeth. He wondered whether she was being truthful, or merely irritating. But then, she didn't know that he loved her, so why would she try to hurt him?

"You don't really mean what you said about having to repay that money, do you?" She was exhausted and leaned against the bed for support. He had to harden his heart, knowing that unless he did he would have to let her go back to her home. And what chance did he have of winning her love if they were miles apart? Besides, if he went to see her in Waterdown, she would probably slam the door in his face.

"I want you to stay here, Claire," he insisted, "for six more months. After that, you are free to go."

She turned around to begin unpacking. "Very well. I have no choice in this matter."

Across the room, Hartley watched her and then because the urge to hold her became so strong, he felt he had to go. As he approached the door and was about the leave the room, she started to speak.

"If you want me to stay here in order to con your business associates for a few more months, I will do that. But, I expect you to play your part."

"Haven't I always?"

"No. I don't believe you have. Now that Miranda is an eligible widow, I suggest you stay away from her."

For one happy moment, he wondered if she was jealous, but then he found out the truth.

"Since you are preventing me from enjoying my life for the next six months, then I'm entitled to do the same to you. Not only that, but I won't be playing the part of a fool for you. You have to end this thing with Miranda."

"Of course," he agreed, and walked out before she could see him smile. Six months with Claire would give him a chance to show her how much he loved her.

If that didn't give her time to grow to love him, then nothing would.

Chapter 12:

Warm rain pattered lightly on the windows but the dark night was hidden by the silk drapes that had been drawn. Claire sat in the living room watching Hartley, who was sitting across from her, reading. It was hard to believe that more than two months had passed since Burnett had passed away. Even harder to believe was how happy she had been with Hartley ever since that time.

There was a subtle change in his attitude towards her. It was difficult to define in words. He seemed less restless now and in the evenings after dinner, when they weren't giving a party or attending one, he was content to sit with her and read or talk. Frequently they listened to music together, or rented movies, or watched a television program. It used to be that Hartley only listened to news or stock reports but that had changed too. He enjoyed watching comedy and laughed easily. It was almost as if they were a genuinely happy couple.

The calm way he had complied with her request not to see Miranda had come as a complete surprise. They occasionally encountered her when they went to social functions but whether Miranda was there at Hartley's request or just on her own, Claire didn't know and didn't ask. She was content with the knowledge that Miranda never came to their home.

This would end soon, she surmised, since they were continuing their marriage in order to staunch the gossip. It would flow again if Miranda was invited to the penthouse. Many times when the phone rang, she picked it up half expecting to hear that throaty voice at the other end. But as the weeks had become one month, and then two, she decided that Hartley must have told Miranda of his promise.

What had her reaction been? Claire wondered. Obviously she must have agreed with the smart idea of avoiding gossip, since on the day of Burnett's funeral she had obviously been too overemotional to think straight.

From the stereo, she listened to the romantic songs from a Diana

Krall compact disc. When the CD was over, Hartley got up to put on another one.

"That was beautiful, wasn't it?" Hartley commented, rummaging through the CD tree for another.

"It was. I love the old songs."

"Let's put on something else in the same vein. How about some early Sinatra?"

"Hartley? Don't put anything else on for a moment. Come and sit down. I'd like to talk with you."

Silently, he sat down again and she marveled – as she did from time to time – at how handsome he was. Honestly, she didn't think he even knew it for his head was in the clouds of corporate big business most of the time. There was a quiet aura about him – he was usually very calm. She could only recall two occasions on which he lost his cool and control. One was the night of Burnett's funeral and the other was the last night in Paris, when they were in her bed together. She pushed that thought aside and started to speak.

"I was thinking that it was time to invite Miranda to dinner," she said. From his expression, she had surprised him.

"Are you sure? The last time you even spoke about her …"

"I was in a bad temper," she finished. "You had forced me to go on with this relationship and I wanted to hurt you."

"And now?"

She shrugged, but didn't reply to him verbally. "I've made out a list of people to whom we owe dinner invitations, and Miranda is on that list." She handed him the page she had printed from her personal computer that afternoon. He glanced at the names.

"Why don't we ask our local member of parliament too? Samuel is eligible and handsome and it might be a good idea to have him on the list."

"Very funny," she said, glad that he noticed that several single males were on the guest list. "You should have been an actor. I almost believed that you were being sincere."

Hartley rubbed his chin thoughtfully and she had the impression that he wanted to say something more but was holding himself in check. She smiled at him.

"Are you finding it hard to put on an act for others?" he asked her softly.

"What?" His question took her by complete surprise but she wanted to answer him honestly. "It hasn't been easy Hartley. I know you've asked me to stay but I also know how much you hate having me here."

"That isn't true! I want to ..."

The telephone cut him short and quickly he answered it. A few clipped words later, he passed it across to Claire. "It's your boy scout," he said sarcastically, but made no move to leave the room when she took the call.

Claire was very sensitive to the fact that Hartley was so close and sounded very stifled and subdued during her telephone conversation. However, she still graciously accepted Jamie's invitation to lunch with him the next day.

"How often do you see him?" Hartley asked as she settled back in her chair.

"About once a week."

"And how often does he call you?"

"What do you care?"

"I'm entitled to know!"

"I don't remember that playing the jealous husband was part of our contractual arrangement. Is it an added clause of your own?"

"Don't make me lose my temper, Claire!" he snapped.

"Then drop this discussion, Hartley!" she yelled. Angry because she was almost in tears, she was intent on hurting him. "You've forced me to stay with you for another six months and I've agreed to those terms. But there is nothing in our arrangement to say that I was not allowed to fall in love with someone else."

"*Have* you fallen in love with someone else?" he demanded

"That is none of your business!"

"Oh yes, it is." He reached out and pulled her to her feet. His hands were like weights on her shoulders and she would have crumpled right back down had he not been supported her body.

"Answer me, damn it!" he continued. "Have you fallen in love with James Farber?"

"Yes, I have!" she cried back. "There, are you satisfied? There is nothing you can do about that."

"We'll see about that." He looked at her sternly and wanted to shake her back and forth. "You are not allowed to go out with him again. Do you understand me?"

She forced a loud short laugh. "I will go out with him whenever I like! You don't scare me!"

"If you do, I will follow you and bring you back home."

"First, this is not my home. Second, you wouldn't dare!"

"Try me," he said, softly. There was a wildness and gleam in his eye that excited her.

"Threats," she taunted. "That's all you seem to be capable of."

"Then I'll give you some action, shall I Claire?" He pulled her close to his body and she let out a breath.

His mouth closed around hers, warm and demanding and she started to struggle free but her strength was so small against his. The pressure of his mouth increased and he sought her moist tongue with his own. He lifted her up until she was standing on the ottoman making her stand face to face with him. It was impossible to move because her body was beginning to betray her; the physical response was telling her one thing as her brain was trying to tell her another. She wanted him so badly; wanted to ask him to take her into his bedroom so they could share sweet release together.

"Claire," he whispered and lightly kissed her along her cheek and down her neck.

His mouth came to rest on the shadowed cleavage between her breasts, and his large hands caressed them gently. His touch was so hot and her desire for him so great that she fairly keened with the want she felt. She clung to him, yet a shred of pride refused to let her submit totally. In the recesses of her mind the name of Miranda still burned and it hurt her. There was no love in Hartley's need of her; only a physical desire which any woman could satisfy for the short term. Sickened by this knowledge, she moved her head away from his and pushed against his chest with her tiny hands.

"Let me go," she cried. "I'm not a substitute for Miranda."

"Claire, don't."

"That's right. Claire won't!" she grimaced, and pushed at him again. "Let me go. I'm saying no to you."

"Please let me show you…" he began.

"No!"

He drew back and, swift as lightening, she was on her feet and at the door. "If you find it so hard to manage without Miranda, you had better make arrangements to go and see her. I would rather you have a physical afternoon with her than have to act as her temporary replacement!"

"That's the last thing I want to do. Claire, please. Listen to me." He was coming towards her. She shook her head and raised a hand to him, fingers splayed.

"Stop right there. Keep away from me, Hartley. If you don't I'll walk out and completely end this. I won't keep my end of the bargain and will move out!"

He stopped and looked at her. "Do you really hate me that much?"

She considered his question and then shook her head. "I feel nothing for you Hartley. Nothing at all."

Quickly she went out and, with her bedroom door closed behind her, leaned for a moment on it, afraid that if she moved away from its support, she would fall down and never be able to get up. Hearing his footsteps behind her, she reached behind and locked her door. So far, she had managed to hide her love for Hartley, but if he touched her again she feared that she would completely give herself to him. She must never do that. If she ever let herself fall, she would never get over it; that's how deep her emotions went. Her tears fell fast and she threw herself onto her bed and buried her face in the soft pillow.

Alone in the living room, Hartley paced the floor, furious with having lost his temper and his control. But anger had flamed his passion and desire for Claire. He had exercised such discipline with his emotions in the past few months and if he didn't continue to do so, Claire would leave him forever.

Throughout the long hours of the night, he lay sleepless with a dull headache behind his eyes, which developed into a severe one by morning. It didn't improve his mood when he entered the dining room and found Claire at the table, looking composed as she always did, leading him to believe that she had given no more thought to him at all and had enjoyed a restful sleep.

The urge to touch her was overwhelming. He longed to feel her delicate bones beneath his fingers; to put his arms around her waist and hold her close to him where she belonged; to breathe in her fresh scent. He wanted to taste her mouth and stroke her soft skin.

But the problem was that she didn't feel she belonged here at all. She had made it painfully clear that she was counting the days until she could walk out of his life. To picture her doing this was anguish, and for the hundredth time he wondered what she would say if he told her he loved her. Last night had been the closest he had been to uttering the words. If that little weasel Jamie hadn't called when he did, he would have done it. Again, he cursed himself for having lost his temper. There were things he said last night that had been guarantees to making Claire leave him forever.

She loved Jamie. How much plainer could she have said it. How defiantly she had turned on him when he forbade her to ever see him again. The knowledge of her falling in love with him was bitter but he tried not to hate the young man. It was just that he believed that he was the only man who could ever make Claire truly happy.

"Claire?" he said aloud. She looked up at him with ice shards in her eyes.

"Hartley. I just want you to know that I'm still planning to have lunch with Jamie today – as arranged."

"I know. I'm sure you would," he said. "I just wanted to say that you have nothing to worry about. I won't follow you and I won't break up your luncheon." He crumpled his napkin and stood up. "Don't bother waiting for me to come home for dinner tonight. I'll be very late."

On his way down to the car, he found that he was shaking and he cursed himself for acting like a love sick fool. He was crazy to let his desire for this little slip of a thing take such a hold over him. He forced himself to remember how much he had loved Miranda a short time ago, and to make himself believe that what he felt for Claire would fade in precisely the same way.

But he knew this was untrue; what he felt for Claire was a more true love as it was one compounded of affection as well as passion. He had grown to like her and to respect her; to appreciate her mind and personality long before he had fallen in love with her. Strange, he didn't even know where the liking ended and the loving began. It seemed that his need of her had always been there. She was the only woman whose integrity he had learned to respect. Even at the height of his passion for Miranda, he never would have trusted her in the same light as he would trust Claire.

Claire – he murmured her name as if it were a prayer, and felt momentary peace enter his head. He couldn't allow her to go out of his life; he would fight for her even if she was in love with another man!

He reached his car and climbed into the back. It was better to take the chauffeur-driven limousine this morning because he didn't trust his scattered mind to focus on driving. As it drew away from the driveway, he settled against the seat and tried to concentrate on his first business appointment. All he could do was to think of Claire.

"Did you say something, sir?" his chauffeur asked, "I didn't quite catch it."

"No, nothing," Hartley muttered. "I was just thinking out loud."

That argument they had last night had shown him that his thinking was getting him nowhere. He had to take action. When he had insisted she remain with him for another six months, he had hoped that, during this time, their relationship would develop sufficiently for him to tell her how he felt. But he had nothing to show for it, except for bitterness. He had to do something. He just didn't know what.

A slim red-haired woman crossed in front of the car at the stop light. She reminded him of Miranda and instantly he knew what had to be done. He had to go to Miranda and tell her that it was over – that he no longer loved her. Only then would he be free to go to

Claire to declare his love. He frowned at the thought of how badly Miranda would take his confession and he cursed himself for not having told her the truth a long time ago.

They had not been alone together since the funeral because Burnett's sister had come from New York and had stayed in the house with her until just last week, making it difficult for Miranda to feel comfortable to be alone with him. It was just as well, he thought, that they hadn't been alone together. The idea of making love to her filled him with shame – even more so now because he saw the whole affair through Claire's eyes. The only good thing he could even say bout his love affair was that Miranda had made the first move towards him. This did not eradicate his guilt; all it did was make it slightly more bearable.

Arriving at the office, he immediately telephoned Miranda to ask if she would be free that evening.

"I'll make myself free," she said, eagerly.

"Don't cancel anything on my behalf," he said quickly. "I'll only be staying a short while."

"Don't be silly, my darling. Joan has left. I'm on my own now. I will expect you to stay to dinner."

"Very well," he said and pretended that Bernadette had come in so he could end their conversation.

Off and on during the day he considered how best to tell Miranda the truth. The prospect of it was daunting and he would rather have faced an irate board of Directors than have to tell her this news. Any woman other than Miranda would already have guessed from his absence and his cold behavior that he no longer loved her. But she had been so spoiled by the men in her life that she could not even fathom her charms ever ceasing to hold their appeal. She no doubt saw their infrequent meeting as part of his plan to maintain the correct status of her recent widowhood. She probably pictured him sitting alone at night in his bedroom, pining for her. This knowledge made him feel even worse. He had been fervent in declaring his endless love for her. Yet here he was, planning to come over to tell her it was all over.

What would have happened if she had come away with him when he first begged her to leave Burnett? Would his love for her have stood the test, or would close proximity have destroyed it even sooner? Certainly there would have been no necessity for the marriage that had brought Claire into his life.

And if he had not met Claire....

He clenched his fist and thumped it on his desk, cursing. Like a dopey teenager, he had mistaken lust for love; had allowed a woman's sexual expertise to blind him to her true character. Disgust closed his throat and nausea gripped him. What a fool he had been!

By six o'clock he was in such a state of nerves that he was almost going to call Miranda to say he couldn't make it. No! He had to tell her the truth, and the sooner the better.

He remained working until the rush-hour traffic had ceased. Because he had dismissed his chauffeur that morning, he drove himself in the Jaguar through the rain-swept streets. Drawing up outside of the house on the Bridle Path, he again gathered his courage and, though he scolded himself for being a coward, he felt that most men in a similar position would be feeling exactly the same way.

It made matters worse to have Miranda greet him with exaggerated affection, one which she generally reserved for when they were completely alone. Tonight she seemed to show no inhibition about displaying her feelings in front of the elderly butler who waited to take his coat.

"Darling! It's been weeks since I've last seen you!"

"No, only about a week. You were at the Robinsons' party last Tuesday."

"I don't count that," she whispered. "I mean it's been ages since we've been alone together."

She linked her arm through his and drew him into the living room. She was still wearing black but it was so low-cut that one was mainly conscious of her pearly skin and abundant cleavage. He had to admit, looking at her, that there had been nothing wrong with his desiring her. She was a beautiful woman. Rather, it was his judgment and action which had been at fault. He should have had the sense to know that physical attraction itself would diminish unless it was accompanied by someone with mental and spiritual attributes as well.

Miranda was not stupid, but he knew that her mind lacked the breadth and cleverness of someone with true intelligence. Again, he was overcome with guilt and self-hatred.

"So, how is Claire?" she asked as she handed him a glass of chilled champagne. "I still cannot understand why you want her to stay on with you. I know you did it for my sake, but honestly I don't care what people say about us. Now that Burnett is gone, we are entitled to take our happiness."

"Don't you feel any blame or guilt at all?" he asked.

"None. Burnett was happy with me until the day he died," she said firmly. "I have no sense of guilt at all."

"I wish I could say the same thing."

"What? You have no reason to feel guilty." Her blue eyes narrowed and stared at him intently.

"No? You think it was easy for me to work for Burnett during the day and make love to his wife in the evening?"

"I wasn't really his wife for years, Hartley. You took nothing away from the marriage in that sense. I gave him all that he would want – all that he was capable of receiving from me – and that was my affection and my companionship." She sat down beside him and snuggled up close. "Darling, please stop thinking about the past. It's all over."

Here was the opportunity he wanted. He opened his mouth but nothing came out. Standing up, he walked over and leaned against the fireplace mantel. "So, what are your plans?" he asked in what he hoped would sound like a casual voice.

"My plans?"

"Yes, Now that Burnett is dead, what are you going to do next?"

"I'm glad you brought that up. It's something we should discuss together. The house is so beautiful and I love it here so I wanted to ask you – do you think it would be better for us to live here than for me to move into your flat?"

"Do you think that's wise?" he burst out and turned so he was facing her directly.

"I think so. I would really love to continue to be living here, but if you prefer that we buy another house together…"

"I don't mean that. I mean our marriage," he interrupted, and waited for his words to penetrate. They did so quickly and it made him wonder if she had guessed that they were coming. Perhaps his aloofness with her since Burnett's death had given her a warning after all.

"Are you saying that you don't want to marry me?" she asked with a low voice.

"I don't think we are right for each other Miranda."

"Spare me that crap! We were perfectly right for each other until a couple of months ago. Or did you only want me when you couldn't have me?"

"I could always *have* you," he reminded her.

"That's rude! I'm not making a sexual reference, and you damn well know it!"

He felt like a mean dog, but continued anyway. "It's the truth," he said. "I have to be truthful with you. I don't love you, Miranda. It has nothing at all to do with Burnett's death. If you really think about it, you will realize that we haven't seen each other much since I got married."

"Well, I assumed that was because you were being cautious. I didn't think it was for any other reason." She shifted her position and the light fell fully on her face. He notice that she had bright spots of red on her cheeks; a sign that she was losing her cool.

"I seem to have been very stupid, haven't I Hartley? Hmm?" Her voice was very quiet and intense. "It occurred to me, of course, that you and I haven't made love since just before Burnett died. I thought it was because you were paying a last respect to him, waiting for a period of time."

"Are you kidding?" he laughed. "After the way I deceived him when he was alive!" Hartley shook his head. "And then after he's dead, I choose to pay him respect finally? That is crazy. When I think of the things we did, the way I acted …"

"Darling, please stop it." She moved swiftly to stand by his side. "You're merely suffering from a temporary attack of conscience. It's making you say things that you don't mean."

"I do mean them. I feel guilty as hell telling you this, but I can't deny my feelings."

"Of course you can." Miranda was calm. "They are not true feelings. You know that we love each other."

"I *don't* love you Miranda. I'm sorry."

The curve of her mouth turned down and it gave her face a hard look. "Is it because of something Claire has said to you? What did she tell you about me?"

"Claire? My God, she has nothing to do with it. I mean….at least she has told me nothing …"

"You love her!" Miranda said, giving each word a measured beat. "Oh my God, you've fallen for my stand-in!" She gave a shrill laugh. "It would be so funny if it weren't so damn pathetic. Brilliant Hartley Dale falling for a little nobody prig like Claire. And why? Because he doesn't need me any more. He used me to get to the top and now he thinks he can stay there all by himself!"

"That's not true, Miranda. I rose to the top on my own merit."

"Baloney! Of course it's true. You're in such denial. You are a ruthless power-seeker. You only wanted me because I was Burnett's wife and because I could put in a good word for you. You used me!"

"Don't you dare minimize what we had together," Hartley protested. "I did love you. If we had married – or if you had left Burnett when I asked you to – things may have worked out differently for us."

"You never loved me!" Miranda retorted. "I was just one more rung on the Farber chairmanship ladder!"

"My love for you had nothing to do with my career," he said softly. "I was willing to give it all up and go back to university if you had come away with me."

"You knew that I'd never do that. Do you think I would have been happy to live on an academic's salary in a university town?"

Miranda started sobbing, her mascara making dark streaks down her cheek. Yet, she still looked so lovely and Hartley was moved by her tears. "Please, let's not say awful things to each other, Miranda. It won't change the truth. It's a pity to spoil what we did have. You are such a beautiful woman and you should marry someone who loves you."

"*You* love me," she cried, her face glistening with tears.

"No. I don't."

"Then it *is* Claire, isn't it?" She looked at Hartley and he nodded. "You're crazy! She'll never be able to give you what I can. She's just a child. I'm a woman!"

"A beautiful woman," he agreed. "I *had* been very happy with you, Miranda. What we felt for each other was not love. It was sexual attraction and excitement. It wouldn't have lasted in the mundane environment of day-to-day married life."

He crossed the door, but she ran forward and blocked the door. "Where are you going?"

"I'm going to the club tonight."

"No! You promised to have dinner with me."

"There's no point in my staying. If I do, we'll only fight. I'm sorry that I've hurt you but there was no other way. It would have been impossible to live a lie."

"You've never lived an honest life! Your whole life is a lie!" She stared at him with fury in her eyes.

Helplessly, Hartley looked back at her, not knowing how to combat her anger or how to lessen her hurt. "I would have given up so much to not have to come here tonight and tell you this. But I can't change the facts."

"So you're going to change women instead?" she screamed. "What will you say to Claire when somebody else takes her place? You'd better be careful about this, Hartley. She won't be as easy to throw in the garbage as me. You are married to her."

Silently, he turned and walked into the hall. Miranda called his name once and he turned to look at her. She was in complete control again, all anger gone, her face and voice calm.

"Burnett has left me all of his shares in the company. If you walk out on me, I will do everything in my power to have you removed from the Board."

A feeling of relief washed over him. He had longed for a way to make amends and here it was, handed to him on a silver platter.

"You won't have to do that, Miranda. I will be resigning from Farber International in the morning."

Flabbergasted, she glared at him. "I suppose you've had a better offer from Watson?"

"Nope. No offer at all."

"You are lying! He's been trying to get you for more than a year. Well, I don't let you go. I'm going to hold you to your contract!"

"I have no contract with Farber," Hartley replied. "But even if I did, nothing would make me continue there. I intend to work for a company where I know that my achievements won't depend on the chair's wife!" He opened the door and slammed it behind him.

Running down the steps, he went to his car and sat behind the wheel, his hands trembling. Only then did he realize how much that little scene had taken out of him. Slowly he drove around the block and parked for some time, waiting until his heart stopped hammering against his ribcage. The pounding in his head continued for some time. Finally, he re-started his car and drove towards his club where no questions would be asked and no talking would be expected. A quick snack and a couple of extra-strength aspirin would make him feel close to normal. Then he would go home and tell Claire that he loved her. That was something he should have done the moment he had felt it.

At this point, it didn't even matter that she didn't love him in return. He was prepared to spend the rest of his life trying to make her change her mind. He didn't care on what terms she stayed with him as long as she stayed.

He sighed heavily. Something else came to the front of his mind. He even loved her enough to give her the freedom she wanted; if that's what it took to prove his love. But, he didn't want to think about her moving out – not tonight.

It would be far better to keep his mind positive. *Keep your eyes on the prize,* Burnett used to say to him.

Claire was a fine prize indeed.

It was only eight-thirty and Claire was restless. It seemed as if the evening had dragged on for hours. Where on earth was Hartley? Not for a moment had she believed his story that he was working late. He was with Miranda. There was no doubt in her mind.

She jumped to her feet and walked around the room again. Far below she could hear the hum of the traffic and see the light of cars moving along the lakeshore. As always, this view thrilled her in its beauty. She knew that she would miss it when she returned to her home town. These past few months with Hartley had served to prove how strong her love for him had grown. It was a love that not even her scorn could destroy. Seeing Jamie today had made this ultimately clear. She would never be able to marry anyone else.

She twisted her wedding ring and watched the diamonds glitter through her tears. What an empty band it was. If only she could turn back the clock to the time when she had never known Hartley. She had been heart-free and full of hope for the future, instead of having no heart to give to anyone else and no future to consider. She felt so empty and sad.

Voices in the hall roused her from her thoughts and, wondering who could be calling at this late hour, she opened the door. Her hands tightened as she saw Miranda.

"I'll keep my coat," Miranda was telling Mary. "I won't be staying long." Bright, blue eyes flashed in Claire's direction. "I took a chance that you would be home."

"Hartley isn't here." Claire was annoyed to find that her voice was trembling.

"Oh, of course I know that, darling," she oozed charm. "I've just seen him at my house."

Automatically, Claire looked over at the front door, and Miranda saw her and smiled. "He's gone to his club for the night. You know what cowards men are. They always rush away and leave their women to do the dirty work for them."

As she spoke, she walked past Claire into the living room and perched on the arm of the sofa, dropping her mink coat from around her. To Claire's astonishment, she looked even more enchanting than ever, thinner since Burnett's death and incredibly beautiful. No wonder Hartley loved her.

"What have you come here for then, Miranda?" she asked quickly. "You obviously have come here to say something."

"I'm not quite sure where to begin," Miranda confessed. "It seemed so easy while I was driving here, but now that we're face-to-face…" Her blue eyes looked beseeching. "Claire, you know I've always been very fond of you --"

"Miranda! Just say what you've come to say!" Claire interrupted, "and cut the charade."

Miranda looked down at the floor and thought for a moment. "Hartley and I want to get married as soon as possible. He has changed his mind about waiting. That's why I've come to see you tonight. He didn't have the heart to tell you himself because he's feeling so guilty. You know, he did insist on you staying with him for another six months – and now he's amended the plan."

"He doesn't have to feel guilty. I offered to leave last night, but he wouldn't let me." Claire managed to get the words out without stammering.

"Yes, well that just goes to show you how guilty he feels. He's afraid that he's ruined your life."

"Not quite as much as he's ruining his own!" Claire said clearly.

"What is that supposed to mean?"

Claire shrugged. "Forget it. I was being too personal. It's none of my business what you two are planning. I'll pack and leave tomorrow."

Miranda glanced at her wrist watch and sighed, looking around the penthouse apartment. "Well, I was thinking …"

"You cannot expect me to pack up and leave tonight!" Claire was incredulous.

"Yes, the idea did cross my mind," Miranda admitted. "As I said,

Hartley is just so embarrassed about it all that I think he was hoping that you would be gone by the time he came home later tonight."

Furious at being kicked out of her home, as she had come to regard it in the recent months, Claire almost lost her temper and started throwing things. But determined not to let Miranda see her out of control, she stayed quiet and waited until her anger eased sufficiently for her to speak again.

"I've already told you that Hartley has no reason to feel guilty," she said calmly. "He knows very well that I want to leave; that's why we had an argument about it last night."

"I know. Hartley hasn't been himself since Burnett died." Miranda's voice was low. "It's been a very difficult time for both of us – but especially for Hartley. He's such a virile man, with a strong appetite and not being able to see me...well, I suppose that it has affected him."

Claire swallowed hard. She was so foolish. She knew what Hartley's love for Miranda had meant to him. But to hear it said out loud affected her more than she could bear.

"I'll leave. I'll leave tonight," she spat out.

"I knew you would be level headed about this," Miranda purred. "I told Hartley that he had nothing to worry about with sensible, little Claire."

With a waft of perfume, Miranda floated back the way she came and left the apartment.

For a long time, Claire stood still in the living room willing herself not to break down in tears. If she started crying, she might never be able to stop. She had to pack and leave quickly, while she still had the strength to do it.

Moving like an automaton, she went to her bedroom. Her cases were stacked in the back of the closet. She pulled them out and began to toss her things into them, not caring in the least if her belongings became creased or crumpled. Back home, she wouldn't have the need for glamorous clothes anyway. Besides, she could probably never bear to wear them again, knowing with what high hopes of making Hartley love her she had bought them in the first place.

She was packing the last of her suitcases when she heard an exclamation behind her and, turning around, saw Hartley standing at the door. She was vividly reminded of the last time she had been packing to leave, though tonight there was a different look on his face and a different urgency to his voice as he stepped quickly into the room and demanded to know what she was doing.

"What does it look like I'm doing?" she asked. "I'm leaving you – as you've requested."

"You're not leaving me! You can't!" He lunged forward and slammed the suitcase shut, again repeating a gesture he had made once before. She was struck by the ridiculousness of the situation. If this wasn't so sad, she might even see how an outsider would find humor in it.

"What is the matter with you, damn it? One minute you ask me to go, and then you act like a bloody maniac when I do!"

"I don't know what you're talking about, Claire!" he said, harshly. "I never asked you to leave!"

"Yes you did! Miranda did it for you, you coward."

"What?" His head tilted as he looked down at her. "What does Miranda have to do with any of this?"

"Everything!" Claire said simply. She re-opened her suitcase and continued to pack. Her hands shook so much that the dress she was holding fell on to the bed. Afraid that if she tried to fold it, it would give away her agitation, she went to her dressing table and pretended to be rummaging with the lotions and perfumes.

"Tell me what Miranda has to do with you leaving?" he repeated, and was suddenly behind her, holding onto her shoulders as he spun her around to face him.

"You dare to ask me that?" she hissed. "You told her to come here. You wanted to save yourself the embarrassment of admitting you had made a mistake in asking me to stay on. Well, if it's any consolation to you, I made a mistake too. I should have left you the day that Burnett died."

"No," Hartley whispered. "I wanted you to stay then and I want you to stay now!"

"Are you planning to start a harem, then?"

"What? Am I planning what?"

"Are you planning to start a harem, with me and Miranda and who knows who else?

"No! I'm planning to start a marriage!" Hartley spat out.

"With who?"

"With *you!*"

He bent down to hug her, but she beat her fists against him and tried to push him away. "You're out of your mind!" she cried, and tried to squirm out of his grasp. "Let me go."

"Never. You're mine Claire and I'm not letting you go. I've been at my club for the last two hours wracking my brain trying to figure out a way to tell you how I feel. I love you! I can't let you walk out of my life."

Her breath caught in her throat and she let it out slowly, afraid that if she breathed too fast, it would make the words disappear and become untrue. She looked at him.

"You love me?" she whispered.

"More than you'll ever fathom. If you leave me, I will have lost the light out of my life."

"But I …No, it can't be true. You've never said…you've never given me a sign."

"I love you," he repeated. "I was afraid to tell you before in case you got frightened and ran away from me. The way you're running away now."

"I'm not running away," Claire looked at him, with an inquisitive look. "You made Miranda come here to tell me to leave."

"No. I didn't. Miranda did that entirely of her own accord. I had no idea that she had come here." His fingers were moving up and down her arms, making her feel light-headed. "I love you, Claire. I believe that I fell in love with you when we were in Paris, but I was too blind to see it. It wasn't until a couple of months ago that I knew for certain."

She still found it hard to accept his declaration of love. "You love Miranda. You can't have changed your mind about that so quickly."

"It wasn't quick. I fought against it. I couldn't believe it was happening to me but those feelings took on a life of their own. You were constantly on my mind. Everything you said; everything you did; the way you looked." His voice was fast and he was blurting out all that he had held inside for so long. "It got so that being with Miranda became a torment. Whenever she came near me, I saw *your* face; heard *your* voice. I thought I was going crazy!"

"I'm not your type, Hartley," she said. "I'm not rich or beautiful or well-connected."

"Stop it!" He gave her a little shake. "Say whatever you like about me, but don't put yourself down any more. You are so beautiful – in a way that Miranda can only dream about. You're rich in compassion and warmth – even though you're not showing much warmth to me!"

"Do you expect me to?"

"No, I don't. Not with the way I've treated you sometimes. But as much as you may hate me, it's nothing with the way I despise my self sometimes." He stepped away from her and raked a hand through his dark hair. "At least you and Miranda have one thing in common. You both hate me."

She ignored the comment. "Miranda said you wanted me to go away, Hartley. That you begged her to come here and tell me to leave at once."

His eyes blazed, their smoky blackness giving the impression of finely polished ebony. "It was the exact opposite. I saw Miranda this evening and told her that we were through. Finished. She took it badly and …"

"I'm not surprised," Claire cut in. "You loved her for more than two years. You only married me so that you could go on seeing her. You can't blame her for being hurt."

"I blame myself!" He put his hand to his temple as if he had developed a severe headache. "I tried to deny my feelings for you, but I couldn't. You made my feelings for Miranda seem tawdry."

Claire sighed. Well, that was the right word to describe his deceitful love affair. She still couldn't forget that it had filled his life for so long. An image of him holding Miranda flashed in her mind.

"You're not the faithful type, are you Hartley? What confidence can I have in a future with you?"

He stood there, nonplussed. "Did Miranda say that to you? For heaven's sake, will I have to spend the rest of my life paying for one mistake? I'm a man, Claire, not a saint. Many men fall in love with the wrong woman, but that doesn't mean they can't then fall in love with the right one! I'm not making excuses," he went on, "but I do want you to see that I'm not the monster you make me out to be. If you want to go and leave me, then do it. But at least let me see you and we can start over, with dating in a normal fashion – and see where it leads from there. I don't care how long I have to wait for you. I just want you to change your mind about me."

Claire looked at him, her stomach fluttering at the excitement she felt. "Time won't make any difference, Hartley. It won't change the way I feel about you."

"I see," he said.

His lower lip trembled and she moved back in order to look up in to his face. His eyes were intent on hers, and she stared into them and saw that they were shimmering with tears. Dismayed, she gave a murmur.

"Don't Hartley. I don't want you to cry."

"Forgive me," he turned his back on her and walked to the door. "Will you at least let me drive you back to Waterdown?"

"I would prefer that you take me back to Paris," she said, smiling. "We never did have a proper honeymoon!"

Slowly he turned, his mouth open as if he did not believe he heard her correctly. The look on her face sent him bounding across the room. Wordlessly, he pulled her close and she felt the warmth of his body and his moist tears as he rested his cheek upon hers.

"Do you mean it?" he asked. "I was so worried because last night you told me you loved Jamie. Now you say ….oh God, Claire. Please let this be true!"

"I don't love Jamie. I love you! When I think of all the time we've wasted…"

"Oh Claire," he said, and covered her cheek with kisses. "I've never met a woman like you. I'm so lucky!"

"And you'll never meet another. I'll never let you go!" She clung to him, her heart soaring.

"I love you so. I'm going to show you the most romantic honeymoon in the world!" He smiled at her, stroking her face with his long fingers.

She laughed out loud, but it was muffled when his mouth covered hers. There was no gentleness in this kiss, just a deep, longing and passionate kiss that made her tremble and turned her lower belly into a warm whirlpool. His hands moved across her back and down her spine, cupping her buttocks with a gentle squeeze. As he held her close to him, she could feel his urgent need of her.

"I love you too, Hartley. Without you, I would be so lost."

His hands moved to the front of her body and he cupped her breasts; he took pleasure in the soft moan that came from her soft pink mouth. "In the morning, I'm going to call the office and tell them that I'll be away for a week. It can't be any longer this time, but once I've resigned from Farber, we will take a proper honeymoon. How does six months touring Europe sound to you?"

"I don't care where we go, as long as we're together." She stroked the back of his neck, savoring the feeling of his hands on her body. "You don't need to resign because of me. I'm not jealous of Miranda any more – I only feel pity for her now."

"I have to leave. I'm so angry at what she did. She nearly came to parting us…" He lowered his head and ran his lips along her earlobe and down her throat to her breast. "I'm planning on spending the rest of my life showing you how much I want you."

"Begin right now," she commanded her voice thick with desire. All she wanted was to make love to him here and now.

"Don't you want to wait until we get to Paris?" he teased.

"No. I can't wait. I want to be with you right now. Then, we can begin again in Paris!"

He kissed her again, his tongue playing softly around the inside of her warm mouth.

She pulled away and looked at him. "And again, and again, and again...."

As he carried her to his bedroom, there was no more need for words. The sweetness of their life together had begun.

Printed in the United States
15669LVS00001B/361-393